SHEEPHERDING MAN

SHEEPHERDING MAN

FRANK RODERUS

DOUBLEDAY & COMPANY, INC.

GARDEN CITY, NEW YORK

1980

All of the characters in this book are fictitious, and any resemblance to actual persons, living or dead, is purely coincidental.

ISBN: 0-385-15570-0
Library of Congress Catalog Card Number 79-7697

99698

For Betty,
with love.

SHEEPHERDING MAN

CHAPTER 1

Most of the time I stay clear of towns, preferring my own company
and that of some animals to most people I've met, but there are
times when I enjoy getting to see some lights and to hear some
noises I haven't made myself. It had been a couple months this time
since I'd seen any sort of town, so I wasn't all that opposed to the
idea. Besides, the fella that wanted to see me must have been
pretty well interested to send a rider three hundred miles after me.
I figured it couldn't hurt to see what the man had to offer.

I got off the train at Evanston and took a moment—like I suppose
most folks do—to marvel at all the Chinese boys in the streets. You
could see more pigtails here than you'd expect to find in a dozen
schoolhouses, and not a one of them on a little girl's head. I'd
heard, of course, that there was a big joss house here, the only one
east of San Francisco, but I hadn't hardly been prepared to hear
more of their birdcall chatter than I heard plain old English on the
streets.

It was interesting enough in its way but not what I'd come here
to see so I picked up my saddle and warbag and hung them over a
shoulder. Beggar came to his feet as soon as I did, his head raised a
bit and cocked to one side, his tongue hanging out the side of his
mouth and his tail twitching just a little as if to tell me he was
ready whenever I was.

I reset my old Stetson and told him, "Come on, boy," and we
went down the street away from the stink and the clatter of the
depot.

A few minutes later we were right back in the same area. Some
clerk-looking fella outside a haberdashery told us Howard Blackburn's office was upstairs over the express office so we'd turned
around and come back. It was a convenient enough location for a
businessman, I suppose, with the tracks in front of the building, the
depot and telegraph office across the street and also against the

tracks and a warehouse to the other side. Having to listen to such noise and commotion all the time would drive me nuts in no time, but then it wasn't my office.

I found the right door, with gold leaf for lettering instead of your common old run-of-the-herd painted sign, and climbed the narrow staircase to another, even fancier doorway.

The stairs creaked and complained with almost every step I took but somehow the man inside the office managed to not hear me coming. He was deep into reading some papers on his desk when I walked in and held the door for Beggar to follow.

The man was medium built and trim enough though he looked like he got too little sun and even less exercise. His hair was going gray and there was less of it than there would have been a dozen years before, more than he would have a dozen years hence. He wasn't bald yet but he had an awful lot of forehead. His coat was hung on a rack in the corner and he was working in his vest and shirtsleeves. Fancy garters around each arm kept his cuffs from being soiled. I didn't have to see his feet under the kneehole of the desk to know he would be wearing low-cut shoes and probably gaiters. His tie was as neat in the late afternoon as if he'd just tied it.

I shoved the door with a boot toe once I was inside and a puff of wind through one of the windows caught it and sailed it shut with a slam. You would have thought I'd fired a gun instead of shut the door.

The man jumped and came bolt upright in his swivel chair. His fingers clawed at the desktop and rumpled a pile of the papers there, and when he looked at me his face lost what little color it normally had.

"You have no business here," he sputtered. He sounded like he was trying to convince himself of that more than convince me. That and maybe run a bluff.

"I kinda thought I did," I told him, not taking offense as he could have no way of knowing who I am.

The man shook his head vigorously and swallowed hard once or twice. "No, I'm sure you are mistaken."

I couldn't help but grin at him. I eased my saddle and gear down to the floor and waggled a finger to point to them. Beggar would be keeping an eye on them anyway but a reminder never hurts. I straightened and said, "You don't know who I want to see but you aren't him, is that it?" He colored a bit at that, and I guess my grin got wider. I took the few steps across the office floor and helped myself to a seat in one of the chairs facing his desk. "I'm looking for Howard Blackburn," I told him.

He cleared his throat and kept eyeing me nervously. "What is it you might want of Mr. Blackburn?"

"Mister," I told him, "if you aren't Blackburn I don't guess it is much of your never-mind just what business I have with the man. If you are him then I figure you are acting awful strange for a man that wanted to see me so bad. I suppose either way it couldn't hurt to tell you my name is Priest."

His eyes narrowed, and he looked me over again but this time with an open skepticism. "How do I know that?" he demanded finally.

Well, I had had about enough of this kind of thing. I got to my feet and out of the corner of my eye I could see old Beggar's head come up. "If you ever see this Blackburn fella tell him I said thanks for the train ride."

I started to turn away and the guy hollered, "Wait!" Well, maybe he didn't actually holler it but he did spit it out pretty quick. I turned and stared at him, deliberately cold but not being nasty about it. Not yet.

"You don't look like my idea of what Jude Priest should look like. You look more like . . . a cowman or something." He acted as if he thought he was kind of insulting me by saying that.

"I used to be a cowhand," I told him. "Still might be if a body could do it alone. It ain't a job I look down on, mister." I was starting to get a little upset with this fellow now, and I guess he could see it starting to cloud up and come stormy.

"Nor would I, I hasten to assure you," he hastened to assure me. He gave me something that might have passed for a smile if you weren't too particular on the subject and leaned across his desk to stick his hand out toward me. "As you no doubt have already concluded, Mr. Priest, I am Howard Blackburn. Thank you for coming, sir."

"Uh huh." I gave the extended hand a look but really didn't feel like shaking it. Instead I signaled Beggar he could lie back down and take it easy and then resumed my seat in the chair facing Blackburn.

He seemed to take no offense to having his hand ignored although I doubt he was much used to the experience. I just figured it could not do a bit of harm to let him know he could not expect me to sit up and beg. He nodded pleasantly enough and sat and said, "I suppose I should not have formed any preconceived ideas about you, Mr. Priest. I apologize. For a few minutes there, well, I thought perhaps you were one of those Cattlemen's Association detectives—or hired thugs and killers, to be more correct about it. I was afraid they had gotten word of my plans somehow and determined to stop me by going to the, uh, heart of the problem, so to speak."

"It makes sense," I agreed, "except then the grangers might figure it a fine way to get rid of *their* problems, too. Some of those old boys are too vulnerable themselves to be passing any ideas around."

"Yes, well . . ." He sat back in his chair and although he did not do it he gave the impression of a man rubbing his hands together and preparing to get down to some serious business. "I suppose you know why I asked you here," he ventured.

"More or less. The details won't matter unless we reach some agreement, of course. But I have a rough idea of what you want."

"They tell me you have been able to go in where others have failed before you."

I couldn't help but laugh, though maybe it came out sounding a little short and even bitter. "Blackburn, *any* fool can go in. The trick is being able to come out again."

A trace of amusement at that pulled his lips straight and thin across his teeth. "Quite so, I am sure, Mr. Priest. Quite so. And your proof is your presence?" I nodded. He went on, "They tell me also that you always stay in as long as you please, that you don't run from trouble."

"It hasn't happened yet," I told him. "I can't say it never will."

He seemed satisfied with that.

"There's something else you better know," I told him.

"Yes?"

"Some folks seem to've got the idea that I'm some kind of hired gun or something."

He looked uncomfortable so I let him squirm in his chair a while until finally he said, "I, uh, heard something like that myself. Frankly I was surprised you have not been hired by the Association."

"They tried," I said, looking him square in the eye, "but what they want for their money is a smoky gun, not a job of work. Blackburn, I'll tell you the same as I've told them. I don't care much for people. Don't much give a damn what they think or say or do so long as it doesn't interfere with whatever I'm doing. Long as I'm left alone I won't bother a soul. Down in Nevada they've mostly figured that out by now so's I can go in anywhere, stay as long as I want and never fire a gun unless I need camp meat. It might could work out that way up here, too, Blackburn. If they leave me be I will repay them in kind. Is that what you want now? If it isn't just say so, and no hard feelings."

Blackburn lowered his eyes and sucked at his teeth, and I could see he was giving it some serious consideration and I was glad. I wouldn't want the man thinking he'd found himself some kind of hired killer here because he had not. Misunderstandings about that could lead to some awful hard feelings down the line, and there was no need for that. At length he looked up and nodded. "You do know there will likely be trouble," he stated. It was not really a question.

"I will not cause it. If I can avoid it and get my job done, I will," I told him.

Again he nodded. "What are your terms, Mr. Priest?"

"What do you offer?" I countered.

He told me, and it was twice what I would have asked. Since it was a first offer he was probably willing to pay more but it didn't seem worth haggling over.

"That will do for the money end of it," I told him. "For the important part of it, Blackburn, there are some other terms. First, you tell me where you want them and when you want them back out. That is *all* you tell me. If you think you've bought yourself a boy we part right here, right now. I go my own way. You supply me with two horses, two mules and an open account wherever you want me to get my supplies here and you send a resupply order once a month. I'll wire when and where it's to be."

"No wagon? No camp helper? Nothing else?"

"No. That's it."

He sucked at his teeth a moment and said, "My secretary has already left for the day. I can have him draw up a contract first thing in the morning."

"No need," I told him. "If we both agree to it, that's enough."

Blackburn's eyes widened. "You would trust me that much?"

It would not be fair to him to give him unpleasant ideas by letting him think he had or could take some advantage here. I gave him a tight little smile and said, "Not so much that I trust you, Howard old hoss, but just about the last thing in the world you'd want to do would be to break your word to me."

He seemed to get the idea all right, and without either of us having to get all hostile about it. That was kinda nice.

"I'll come back by in the morning then. You can have your instructions ready for where and when I pick up the beasts and where you want me to stock up. Oh yeah, make sure they've all been dipped before I get them. I want them tick free and healthy as possible going in. Otherwise I'll have a devil of a time putting weight on them with as much moving as I may have to do."

This time he did look startled. "Do you mean you actually expect to show a gain on the flock from this?"

"Mister, you are hiring me to herd your sheep, aren't you? Well I've always kinda had it in mind that the idea behind tending any kind of livestock was to improve them so you can show a profit on them. And, mister, if I can't give you a gain in weight, why, I'll not have done a very good job, will I?"

He shook his head and I almost laughed at him but did not. Hell, I was serious too. I figured to take those woollies into Thunder Basin, graze them there and put a gain on them, then fetch them out again. There hadn't been sheep there before, and maybe the cow outfits would have trouble adjusting to the idea of there being sheep on the public grass, but there was really no reason it shouldn't work out just fine for everybody. Just as long as they left me alone with my woollies I would leave them be too. If they didn't, well, we'd work it out somehow.

I stood and clucked to Beggar and nodded a good-bye to Howard Blackburn.

"Everything will be ready by late morning," he promised.

I grunted and took up my saddle and warbag. I headed down the stairs with Beggar beside me and a mostly satisfied but partly confused wool grower in the office behind us.

Actually, well I guess he had a right to be looking so uncertain about us—me—because neither Beggar nor me looks like much.

Beggar now, he just is not what most folks think of when a sheep dog is mentioned. Nor is he so much a sheep dog as just plain good dog. He is large and stocky built with heavy chest and shoulders and a broad, massive head. His hair is short and slick, a liver brown in color. A good bit of his tail is missing and his ears have been chewed and clawed some shorter than they used to be. His eyes are pale, almost a pinkish tan. He has enough scars on his head and body to give him a rough and downright mean appearance, and the truth is that Beggar is a helluva lot rougher and meaner than he looks. He got his name mostly because even as a pup he was too independent and ornery to ever have to beg for anything.

Me, well I don't hardly know what to say. There are plenty of bigger men around though I'm a shade above average in height, I would say. Built for speed and staying power instead of Beggar's blocky, bull-like power. My hair is a light brown and my eyes, like Beggar's, quite pale. I have regular features and usually am not considered too homely. At least the ladies do not seem to think so.

Women are usually a little cautious of me for some reason, though I try always to be polite and use a gentle touch. Many of them seem to find me cold, and of course they are entitled to their opinion. I have no basis for comparison myself.

Anyway, to get back to the matter at hand here, I guess I do dress like a cowhand rather than a sheepherder—which is only to be expected since most people's idea of a sheepherder would be a Mexican or a Basque—and while I do wear a gun I wear it like anyone else would, holstered at my waist and not slung low or tied down or any such show-off foolishness.

Blackburn must not have been put off by what he saw or he would not have hired me. And really I did not much care one way or another. If someone was willing to pay me to stay out away from the towns I would take the money and do the work. If not, Beggar and I would stay out on our own until we did find work. It just didn't matter that much to me, either way.

So I took Howard Blackburn's job and headed on down into the street to find some entertainment and spend the hour or so it would take before I would have had a complete bellyful of town and people and be anxious to get out away from them again.

CHAPTER 2

Now I was feeling peaceful enough when Beggar and I hit the street level again and stood for a moment on the graying wood of the walkway in front of Blackburn's downstairs door. I set my saddle down and thought about firing my pipe to take the taste of the train ride out of my mouth. Beggar sat patiently beside me.

He shifted to attention a moment later and came to his feet with his teeth bared. I could feel more than hear his low, warning vibration of a growl as he stood there against my leg.

I stepped out a bit away from my saddle and bag so they would not be in the way. There were a couple big old boys crossing the dirt of the street toward us and from the expressions they wore and the intent way they were staring I would say that Beggar had been right in his warning.

Both of them were what you might call town-type plug-uglies, dressed like railroaders or some such sort in lace-up shoes and city britches with suspenders instead of belts and flannel shirts open at the throat and a long way from the last washing. If there was a town ordinance against the wearing of guns I hadn't noticed it before, but these two were walking bare as far as I could tell. But then they looked rough enough to think they wouldn't need such help.

More interesting, considering where I'd just come from, was a man standing back under an awning on the far corner where these two had just been. I couldn't tell all that much about him in the shadows there but I could see enough to tell that he was dressed neatly, much better than either of these boys, and was wearing a wide-brimmed hat that looked like a horse ought to be under it. I guess I smiled just a little before I shifted around to face them square on.

The two of them stepped up onto the boards and stopped in

front of me. Close up they didn't look a bit better than they had at the distance.

One was a couple inches taller than the other, who looked like he was a few pounds heavier in spite of that, but even so it would have been hard to tell them apart. Both were wearing soft, cloth caps and when the taller one lifted his to scratch he showed a bald spot. Maybe that was the way one was supposed to be told from the other, I decided. If anyone wanted to bother ever. I did not figure I would care all that much.

Baldy finished scratching and tugged his cap down in place. He gave me a grin that I suppose was intended to be wicked, maybe even frightening, and said, "You're about half ugly, aren't you?"

"Then that still gives me a leg up on you by twice as much," I told him. He didn't react to that at all. I said, "If there's something you want, spit it out. Otherwise leave me alone. I'm really not in a mood to be bothered."

Baldy looked at his friend and snickered. "He doesn't want to be bothered, Tim. What do you think of that?"

"Not very friendly," Tim judged. "I'd say he needs mannering. Maybe a reminder."

"Boys," I warned them, "I am not exactly new to what you are trying to do here. You aren't going to teach me anything. You aren't going to change my mind about anything. You might even be very rudely surprised. I don't hold with the idea of letting myself be thumped on by morons. Now save yourselves some trouble. Go back to your friend over there and tell him it won't work."

Baldy managed to look affronted. "We don't have a notion of what you mean," he declared.

"Bull!"

He shrugged and half turned toward Tim as if he was about to say something. He went ahead and made his hand into a hoof-sized fist while he was still turning away, though.

Well, there wasn't much I could do about it. It was a stupid game someone wanted to play. The fellow across the street had probably spent ten or twenty dollars to learn something, but these two fine boys were going to have to pay the heavier price for him.

Tim was standing on the left so I knew I didn't have to worry about him. When Baldy started to turn back my way—and a neat, sure pivot it was, too—his right was coming up in a straight, hard line from his shoulder toward my jaw. If I'd been foolish enough to let it land it would have been right effective, I'm sure. It didn't.

I dipped my knees and let his fist whistle by overhead. He'd thrown it good and hard and it left him off balance. I straightened and gave him my knuckles in the soft hollow under his arm. Or in what should have been a soft place. On him it was solid enough that I hadn't hurt him a bit.

He wasn't any slow-thinking slouch at what he did, either. His right was still way out there and he whipped it around backhanded against my head and set my right ear to ringing like Sunday morning in St. Louis. Lots of bells.

Baldy squared off with me then and kind of grinned. I would have sworn he was pleased as a body could be that I wasn't going to roll belly up and let him do as he liked without a decent scrap.

He feinted with his left and I ignored it, and he grinned all the wider.

He tried another little item then. Tried to plant a boot toe in my crotch, which I did not appreciate. I managed to take it on the thigh instead but even so it hurt like hell and made me mad, which I hadn't been until then.

Baldy stepped back and looked at me. He seemed to have forgotten that he wasn't supposed to be alone in this fight but the low sounds Beggar makes when he is busy that way told me that this man was quite alone here.

I nodded to him and motioned him forward.

He put his hands up like a prize fighter and came toward me, sort of high and bouncy on his toes and shuffling ahead without losing much contact with the ground as he moved.

I blocked a quick left, slipped aside from the right that followed and looped one over his shoulder to the throat. That one had to hurt him. He went a little white in the face and was having trouble breathing.

I wasn't in this for sport, and Baldy had already extended the invitation. I shifted my weight onto my left foot and when he staggered a bit he left his near leg straight for a moment with the heel of his shoe planted on the board sidewalk. The opportunity seemed right so I kicked him on the knee joint. The loud pop I heard before Baldy screamed told me that it was at least dislocated if it wasn't busted.

He went down howling, and it took me a moment to get Beggar's attention over all the noise the man was making.

By then Beggar's little piece of the sidewalk was getting red and slippery, and I wasn't at all sure that anyone was going to be able to repair the man Baldy had called Tim.

Beggar was still trembling and ready but he pulled back beside me where he belonged.

By then—way too late—there were some people running toward us yammering noisily, about half of them trying to take charge or to tell the others what they had seen happen.

Finally I saw one wearing a badge. I told him it looked like a strong-arm robbery attempt, and he seemed satisfied with that. Once I'd told him that he didn't seem really very interested anymore.

"You're all right?" he asked like he really didn't care anyway.

"Sure." It was true enough. My ear wasn't ringing anymore and I checked and couldn't find any blood there, so Baldy hadn't done any damage with that backhanded slap.

"You can follow me over to the office and make out a complaint," the badge-toter offered.

I shrugged. "No point in it. The town would just have to pay to mend them."

He didn't argue, just quit pretending the interest he seemed to have felt obligated to give.

"You could tell me something, though," I said.

The deputy grunted. He looked a little annoyed now.

"Where could I find a public trough or pump?"

He never even asked why. "Up to the corner there and turn right a block."

I thanked him, picked up my gear and walked away. The crowd that was still milling around parted so easy I almost got an idea of how Moses must have felt with the waters opening up in front of him.

Not that I had anything to do with that. I don't think there was a one of those people who could have told a friend what I looked like five minutes afterward. But I'll just bet they could have given a hair-by-hair description of old Beggar. With all the gore on his coat he looked even meaner than usual and was the center of attention.

We hiked up the street in the direction the deputy had pointed and turned out of sight of the crowd that was still lumped on the corner near Blackburn's office. There was no sight of the big-hatted man who had been standing across the street.

I found the water trough all right and told Beggar to sit. He was calm now and seemed to enjoy the bath I gave him. He wasn't fit to be seen in polite society the way he had been.

CHAPTER 3

There is something about a railroad town that gravels me more than most places will anyhow, and recent events had not made me feel any better about it. I suppose it is the noise. All that hissing and clanking, ringing bells and idiots yanking the pulls of steam whistles and other idiots using hammers to beat on loud metal. Railroads stink, too. Hot grease and live steam and the heavy smell of burned cinder that will stay in a body's hair and clothes for days after riding the cars. Other people have told me they can't smell it for so long, but I can. Don't like it either.

So when I left Blackburn's office I walked away from the tracks as far as I could go and still find a boardinghouse. The hotel was too close to the depot to be of interest except as a last resort.

My saddle and bag were commencing to feel heavy so I was ready enough to stop when I found a narrow, two-story clapboard house with a sign hung out front saying "Guests." I set my gear on the edge of the porch and motioned Beggar to guard it before I knocked on the door. A middle-aged woman answered the knock.

"Evening, ma'am," I told her. "I'm looking for a room. Something with some peace an' quiet to it."

She gave me a careful eyeballing before she nodded. "Dollar for the room. Fifty cents a meal. I don't put up with any rowdying."

"That's fine, ma'am. Neither do I."

"Is that your dog?"

"Yes, ma'am. He goes wherever I do. If that's any problem for you I'll take him somewhere else."

"He looks mean."

"Yes'm, but he won't bother anybody unless he's supposed to."

"What does that mean?"

I grinned. "It means your other boarders won't bother my gear while I'm here, ma'am."

"Hmmph. I could use a dog like that myself." She swung the

door wide and stepped back. "Come on in, then. You can have the front room. Up the stairs and turn right. Supper in an hour. I only call them to dinner the once."

"Yes, ma'am." I got my things and went up.

The room was all right. It had a cot and a washstand and a little table for piling stuff on. There were some hooks in one corner and a curtain hung on a wire across another corner. It was the sort of place that would cater to married men or quiet-living bachelors doing temporary work away from home. She probably drew a fair trade from the railroad people. I stretched out on the cot to wait for the chow call.

There was a lock on the door but no key so when she hollered I left Beggar to keep an eye on things and went down.

The dining room sure wasn't crowded. There were only three others at the table, not counting the woman, who was loading the table but apparently not sitting to it. The three men were town-type workingmen in overalls and little soft-billed caps. They gave me a stare when I came in, but they didn't say anything.

The food was town stuff, too, which is one of the few good reasons a man might have for putting up with the places. The woman had fixed ham and some leatherbritches cooked in ham juice and there were mashed potatoes. There were fresh peaches on the table and peach cobbler for dessert. Like I said, a man's belly *can* admit to some advantages in being close to town and trans-portation. Anyway, I enjoyed what the woman had fixed, and I told her so.

She snorted and frowned like she didn't believe a word I said but when I turned to leave she offered, "Don't be in such a hurry now. I'll fix a pan of scraps for the dog. But mind you bring my pan back, you hear?"

"I will," I told her, and I did.

After dinner there didn't seem much point in sitting inside four walls with nothing fresh to read so I lighted one of the wall lamps and turned it down low and left Beggar to guard my gear in case anyone should come calling.

It was coming dark and most of the town was closed up, but down along the tracks there were some entertainment emporiums that would stay open as long as there were customers who had tastes they wanted catered to. I drifted down that way and loafed on the street corners a while until I decided which of the places might be the least objectionable.

The quietest seemed to be a little hole-in-the-wall outfit on a side street near the stock shipping pens. There weren't so many loud-mouthed railroaders going in and out of that one so I went inside and settled at a little-bitty table in a back corner. There were only three tables in the place and none of the others was occupied. There were a handful of fellows in range clothes at the bar.

The barkeeper did not look overjoyed to have a customer he'd have to walk out to wait on but he didn't make any fuss about it. He didn't come out to wait on me either, so eventually I wandered over to the bar and asked for a beer. He drew one and took my dime without getting chatty about it, which was just fine by me.

Some hinge-jawed yahoo standing next to me, though, seemed to think the only reason a man might want to go into a bar would be to listen to some other idiot's problems. He started trying to tell me how rough he had it with whatever outfit it was he drew pay from —I wouldn't go so far as to expect that he worked there—but I figured the polite thing to do would be to avoid pointing out that it couldn't have been too rough if he had time for a night in town in the middle of the week. I turned and carried my beer back to the table, leaving him standing there talking at the air where I'd been.

I buried my nose in the suds and when I looked up damned if this same fella wasn't in front of me again. He looked kind of provoked and had enough red in his face to make me wonder how long he'd been standing at the bar sopping it up.

He set his mug onto my table and said, "You shouldn't oughta walk away from a man when he's talking to you."

I gave him a closer look and still didn't see anything that would make him look interesting to me. He was an ordinary-enough fellow and still had the thong looped over the hammer of his revolver. The existence of the revolver answered the question about the gun ordinance. The thong would keep the thing from coming out of the holster by accident. It also keeps them from coming out on purpose unless you slip it free ahead of time. Me, I don't have such a thong on my holster. I'd rather lose a bucketful of guns than one gun fight, and I've never figured myself bright enough to always know ahead of time when a man might have some serious need of the difference. You wouldn't have to be wrong but once to make yourself sorry. Anyway, it was kind of interesting to see that this fellow wasn't all that serious yet. I gave him a looking at and went back to my beer.

"I was talking to you, mister."

I took another swallow.

"Are you going to answer me or do I have to beat hell out of you to get your attention?"

You had to give him credit for persistence, but this really was getting tiresome. Neither of us had ever before laid eyes on the other, I was sure, and he didn't look either all that drunk or all that proddy. Before I went up to the bar this fellow'd been having a quiet conversation with another man. He hadn't been loud nor seemed especially belligerent then.

I looked past him toward the bar. The other man was still there, propped with one elbow on the bar and keeping his eyes on me and the annoyance. That one was somewhat better dressed than this fellow and wore his gun tied down onto his thigh. I couldn't be sure, but he might well have been the fellow under that awning earlier. He had a thong on his holster too but it wasn't in use now. I raised an eyebrow in his direction, and he grinned and said something to the bartender. The man picked up his mug—not with his gun hand, I noticed—and ambled back to join me and his feisty friend.

"It's all right, Jack. Go on back to the bar and have yourself a drink. Anything you want is on me tonight."

Jack bobbed his head, gave me another hard look and carried his beer back to the bar.

The other man smiled and asked, "Mind if I sit?"

I shrugged and nodded toward a chair. I had not been looking for company but this fellow had managed to get my curiosity up. He sat back in the chair with his hands in plain sight and took a small sip of his drink and gave me time to look him over.

He was slender and not above average height but he had a quick and competent look about him. He was clean-shaven and freshly barbered and his clothes were neatly fitted and clean. He was wearing dark trousers and a vest that matched them and a soft brown shirt that looked comfortable. His boots were brown and freshly waxed and of a color that matched his gunbelt. His hat was a dark brown nearly the same shade as his leather. Neat, like I said, but without giving any impression that he was some kind of dandy. He looked more like a competent individual who also happened to be quite tidy about himself. His eyes were a light blue-gray not dissimilar from my own.

When I'd had ample time to look him over—and him to return the treatment—he asked, "Where's the dog?"

If he was expecting to draw some sort of reaction out of me with the question I imagine he was disappointed. I've no interest in the game but they tell me I have a good poker face. "He's working tonight," I told the fellow.

"Buy you a refill?" he offered.

I nodded and he went to fetch two more mugs. I did not notice him saying anything to Jack while he was over there.

When he came back he set the beers down and slipped the thong over the hammer of his Colt before he resumed his seat. "Not very talkative, are you?"

"Not generally."

"That implies there can be exceptions to the rule."

I waited for him to come to the point. It was getting farther past the dinner hour now and the place was starting to fill up. I kept an eye on the rest of the room while I waited. If I'd been him I would have been more than a little uncomfortable with my back to so many strangers.

"I noticed you coming out of Howard Blackburn's office earlier," he said.

"So did half the town."

He took a swallow of his drink and said, "You don't look much like a sheepherder. The dog doesn't look much like a sheep dog, either."

"I could say you don't look much like an Association man, but it wouldn't hardly be the truth."

He laughed. "You have it, all right. Range management division."

"That's what they're calling it these days?" I was genuinely curious. It had been some time since I'd been up this way, and I'd never really spent much time here. Just passing through once.

"Yes. Range management. That is very important, you know. Men like Howard Blackburn, now. They don't seem to understand the importance. They seem to think our investigative division is down on them. Not so," he said easily. He spread his palms in a gesture of innocence. "These sheep men, why they've done absolutely nothing of interest to the detectives. They aren't thieves, you know. They have every right to run stock on the public domain, just as we have. Range management's interest is simply to preserve the quality of grazing, for the benefit of all, beef and wool growers alike."

"Uh huh." Talk like that would sound real good in the news-papers and when the lobbyists got to talking in Cheyenne. I had to admire the logic of it. I didn't believe a word of it, of course, but I did have to admire the logic.

"Blackburn doesn't seem to understand that," he went on, "but I certainly hope you can appreciate our position."

The man was more than a neat dresser. That was as neatly worded a threat as I had ever heard. "I believe I do, Mr. . . . ?"

He smiled. "Richard Brock," he said, extending his hand.

I took his hand to shake and said, "Priest. Judas Priest."

Frown lines tugged briefly at the corners of his mouth, and I got the impression he very nearly repeated my name as an exclamation. His grip tightened involuntarily for a moment before he released my hand. I could not help but smile a little.

He looked—if I may be forgiven the pun—a bit sheepish. "You are not, uh, entirely unknown to us, Priest."

"You can call me Jude if you like."

He nodded. "I apologize, Jude. If I'd known, well, I wouldn't have played these silly games with you."

"No harm done. Not to me anyway."

"Can we be straight with each other, Jude?"

I grinned at him. "I thought we were being straight, Brock."

He showed it very little but I got the impression he was more than a little unsettled now. "Look, Jude, I don't know what your arrangement with Blackburn is, but I'm sure the Association would, uh, compensate you adequately if you were to, well, to reconsider."

He was coming close to being annoying now, and I guess my grinning good humor got lost there. I could read in his eyes that he noticed the change. "Go back and look at your files again, Brock. It likely says that I can't be bought. In fact, it would make me really unhappy if anyone tried. I hope you wouldn't do that."

Brock looked like an unhappy man himself. He pushed himself away from the table and stood, leaving his second beer untouched and most of his first still in the mug. "I won't ask when you're going. Or where. You will understand, of course, if I keep an eye on you."

"Of course," I told him. "Hell, you're welcome to come along and give me a hand if you like. Or wouldn't the Association understand that?"

"I think perhaps they would not."

I nodded. "See you in the morning, Richard."

"Yes, well . . . good night." He left the bar without stopping to say good-bye to Jack and the other cowhands at the bar. I hoped he would get a good night's rest. I kind of liked Richard Brock.

CHAPTER 4

"You were seen talking with an Association detective last night," Blackburn accused as soon as I walked through his office door. His voice was icy cold and his manner was a whole lot more confident than it had been the day before. His secretary might have had something to do with that. The man seated at the second desk was a head taller than me and seemed to have about as much muscle as your average black bear. And even though he was wearing his coat in the office it was pretty plain that he had a well-filled shoulder holster under there. He seemed to be a double-duty sort of employee.

"Sure was," I said agreeably. I nodded to the secretary and plopped myself into the chair in front of Blackburn's desk. It wouldn't likely be necessary but I tilted a finger toward the secretary. I don't think either man noticed it, but Beggar did. He sat down beside me with his tongue out, looking dumb and happy, but if the brawny ol' boy at the other desk made the wrong jump he would have himself a face full of dog. "He said his name was Richard Brock. Do you know him?"

Blackburn grimaced. "I know the type. Hired killers every one. What would he want with you?"

"That's kinda obvious, isn't it? He wanted to buy me off or at least find out where you intend to move."

"What did you tell him?"

"Why, I invited him to come along and help."

"You *what?*"

I laughed into Howard Blackburn's reddening face. "Of course. He's gonna follow anyway. There's no way you can hide a couple carloads of woollies. The man might as well make himself useful as skulk around in the shadows, 'specially since I'll know he's there anyway."

"Surely he is not going to do it."

"No, I don't think so. Said he didn't believe the Association would approve."

Blackburn shook his head. "It is damned seldom that I agree with the Association about anything, but this time I certainly do. I will accept your version of what happened, Priest. This time. I do not want you consorting with Association people in the future, however. Is that clear?"

"It would just amaze you, Howard, to know how little I care about what you think or what you want." The secretary's attention began to focus my way, and down by my side old Beggar gathered his feet under him and clomped his jaw shut at the change in the man's manner. "I thought we'd worked that out yesterday, Howard. If you want to change your mind now just say the word. I can find all the work I want down in Nevada."

Blackburn managed to swallow away his inclination toward bossiness. He gave me a weak smile and shook his head. It was enough to make me wonder how many sheep and how many herders he'd already lost trying to get a toehold on the free grass the Association claimed as their own private part of the public domain. I very strongly got the impression there were some things that Howard wasn't telling me, but I sure didn't know what. "No, I . . . forgot for a moment there," he said.

"No harm done. Do you have that list of instructions for me? And the authorizations I'll need?"

"Yes. Of course. Ronald?" He held out a hand and the secretary went back to being interested in office matters. He found the correct packet of papers and carried them to Blackburn. His boss took them without acknowledgment and shoved them across the desk to me.

I nodded and took my time about reading them over. When I was done I nodded again and said, "That seems to be about it then. How long will it take to have the sheep dipped and ready for transport?"

"They were dipped last night. I've reserved car space through to the first Nebraska siding. You can trail them north from there unless you want to route all the way around and come down from Montana."

I grinned at him. "Let's save you some mileage cost on those cars, Howard. You aren't going to fool anybody by using a side door anyway. So I think I'll just offload in Cheyenne and drive them from there. Might be kinda fun."

"Judas Priest!" the secretary blurted. "That's the hornets' own nest over there."

"Ain't it, though," I agreed. "And I do wish you wouldn't use my name like a cuss word. A fella gets kind of tired of that, you know."

I was satisfied enough with Blackburn's arrangements and downright pleased with his woollies. He hadn't given me any smooth-mouthed old ewes with their teeth worn away and them ready to die already, even though such a flock would have been a smaller loss for him if the Association managed to destroy them. What I had were a thousand young wethers already castrated and well weaned, ready to double their size and their value once they hit the rich, free grass of the open country. I liked that. And he hadn't left me open to trampling losses at the outset by shoehorning them into two cars but hired three stock cars. The center car had an area partitioned off for my horses and gear. He hadn't been able to come up with any decent mules and had given me pack horses instead, but they looked to be good ones and I offered no objection.

The saddle horses were definitely good ones. Short-coupled, blocky animals with straight legs and good necks and finely molded heads. You will generally find that a good-made horse is a good moving horse as well, and I liked both of these when I tried them. One was a deep sorrel, the other a blue roan so dark he was nearly black. The blue horse looked to be about as tough as forged iron. As a precaution against any legal maneuvering by the Association, Blackburn had made over bills of sale to me on all four horses and was holding postdated bills of sale conveying them back to him. That little detail had been his idea, and it was a good one. More than one herder has been hanged as a horse thief when what he'd really done was take sheep onto beef ground.

I loaded the sheep late in the afternoon, and the train was made up a couple hours later. I told Beggar to guard and stepped into the depot. Sure enough, Brock was perched on one of the benches where he had a good view through the tall windows. He had his saddle and warbag by his feet.

"You'd best get aboard now," I told him. "It would be a shame if you missed the train."

He gave me a narrow-eyed look and said, "Surely you don't expect me to fall for this. I don't know how or where you're going, Priest, but I sure have the idea it won't be on this train. Those weren't any worthless grassbusters you loaded. Those are young, healthy lambs. Blackburn wouldn't want to lose them. Besides, I know what the lading on them claims. That is kind of insulting, don't you think? Cheyenne? Give me credit for more sense than that, man."

I grinned at him. "Suit yourself. Of course your employers are going to be awful mad if you guess wrong. And I want you to remember, Brock. I've been decent enough to warn you the train is ready to pull out soon."

They already had steam up and through the open windows we could hear the hiss bleeding out through the escape valves. A conductor began bawling a last call by the passenger coaches. If Brock was going to board he'd best do it soon, but he seemed to have convinced himself I was going to jump off at the last second, when he would be in a passenger coach and not be able to see. He gave me a tight little smile and shook his head.

Well, nobody had gone and appointed me his keeper. There was no way I could keep the Association from finding out where I took those woollies. Sooner or later they would know anyway so it seemed kind of silly to play games about it, and if Brock wasn't spying on me and working against me one of their other people would be. Like I said, though, it was up to him what he wanted to believe. I fingered my hat brim in a little salute and ran back along the length of the train toward my stock cars.

A whistle shrieked when I was halfway there and the couplings began to crash as the engine eased ahead to take up the slack between the cars. Someone fed power to the man-tall driving wheels and the train began to glide forward. I swung through the open door beside Beggar without seeing Brock quit the depot.

If he absolutely insisted on outsmarting me he was certainly entitled to try. So I chuckled a bit to myself and rolled out of sight behind the sliding door before the car passed the depot windows where he would be watching. That would be one highly angrified fellow when he found out he'd been had after all. It was comfortable enough right where I was lying so I tugged my hat down over my eyes and laughed myself to sleep.

CHAPTER 5

Cheyenne at daybreak was not as disgustingly busy as a city normally is so as soon as the wethers were offloaded into the pens I pushed the gate wide and swung my arm. Beggar got busy in his quiet, workmanlike way, nipping at their heels and giving orders in short, breathless little yips to shape the flock into a bunch and stream them out onto the public roadway.

Just for the hell of it I marched my bleating woollies smack downtown and turned them north toward the capitol building. I would have to say that we attracted some awfully curious looks from the early risers among the city's businessmen, and outside the newspaper office a shirt-sleeved gentleman with a coffee cup forgotten in one hand and a wad of blank paper in the other came out and demanded to know what I was doing. I told him—more or less—but I don't know if he ever printed any of it. He looked more mad at the affront of seeing sheep on the streets than curious about the reasoning, and I hoped Howard Blackburn was not counting on any editorial outcry in behalf of sheepmen's rights. I didn't hardly think this fellow believed mutton eaters had rights. But I noticed he was wearing wool pants.

The capitol building was imposing enough to satisfy the most discriminating taxpayer, I thought, but I was disappointed that I didn't know where I could find the cattlemen's famous clubhouse. If I'd known where it was I would have driven by it and maybe had Beggar stir the wethers into a little noise.

As it was we passed enough well-dressed gentlemen to pretty much assure that the telegraph wires would be smoking hot with messages for Richard Brock. I could not say that I was real unhappy thinking about that.

I had never worked this far north and east before, and I must say that I was pleasantly surprised. Farther south, in Nevada and Arizona, where I had spent most of my time the past ten years or so since I left my home grounds at nineteen, the forage is of good quality but can get awfully seldom. There is an awful lot of wide country there where you can find a bunch of bare ground between the bits of edible greenery.

I pretty much expected Wyoming to be the same and what little of it I had seen before was open and empty and mostly barren, as I was used to. This country north and east of Cheyenne, though, was enough to make a stockman—sheep or beef, I don't care which—quiver just from looking at it.

The grass was like a carpet, thick and rich and beautiful and rolling on for mile after mile, and it seemed that the farther I traveled the better and fuller it got. I began to understand for the first time how this land could have supported the big buffalo herds I'd heard about but never saw before they were gone and the opportunity was lost forever. Until I saw this grass I was always skeptical about the reports of those old herds. Now I wasn't so ready to argue. This was country the likes of which I had not imagined before, and I could not blame the cowmen for being jealously possessive of it. Had there been trees here too I would have been tempted to take up a claim on it, even knowing that a man cannot survive here on a quarter-section homestead. The truth is, though, that I am a man that needs the sight and the feel of trees around him also and so for day after day I pushed my flock of wethers through this grass and each day of that time I was in admiring awe of this country I traveled.

I drove north and east from Cheyenne, staying clear of the old Deadwood stage road, and the broad grass swallowed me and my animals. There were few enough people here so that by crossing rather than following the watercourses it was no great trick to avoid meeting anyone.

Once the sheep were used to the routine Beggar and I had but little work to do. With no ewes in the flock we did not have to concern ourselves with lambing, and of course there is little doctoring or tending to be done if you have no new lambs. There is practically no such thing as a sick sheep anyway. They are either live or dead, and I cannot quarrel with the old saying that a sheep is just an animal in search of a place to die. Still, these were young and healthy wethers and so we were having no losses.

For camp meat I shot an occasional antelope from among the herds that were so common and that seemed so curious about the woollies. Beggar mostly fed himself from the jackrabbit population.

I enjoyed that time and it lasted through five days of clear skies and starlit nights until the cattlemen found us. When they did it was not Brock or some others of the Association people but a local crew who had heard too much about feuding and seemed to think it a sport instead of the serious business it really is.

I saw the first of them early in the morning. He topped a rise not more than a mile away and straight in the path of our travel. He dropped back to the other side of the grassy knoll almost immediately but for several minutes I could see a small dot against the sky that meant he was still there looking us over.

"Play time is over, boy," I told Beggar. "I think it's about time we have to start earning our keep."

I let Beggar take the flock ahead while I stopped to shift my saddle from the sorrel to the blue horse. I had already learned that the roan was the steadier under the sound of gunfire. The sorrel was not panicked by the noise but tended to fidget and paw while the blue would stand firm. The sorrel was the faster of the two, but I did not intend to do any running.

Nor did I intend to turn the flock to another line of travel. Sheep and race horses are not close kin and once spotted we could be caught by anyone who chose to follow. I made the saddle switch and resumed my place behind the slow-moving flock.

A couple hours later we were crossing another of those undulating rises when I saw three riders coming at a canter from the east. They were several miles away and closing steadily. I let out a short bark to get Beggar's attention and swung my arm. He gave a little yip and raced toward the head of the flock to turn them in on themselves. Between his scampering harassment and some quick-footed work by the roan we had the wethers close-bunched and quiet long before the cowboys drew near.

There were three of them, like I said, all of them young and lean and with laugh wrinkles at their eyes. They rode your average, scrubby using horses, each of them probably taken from the rough string and used with as much stubborn pride as with skill. They looked like good boys on those horses and once I had been much like them, but they all wore guns at their belts and they might wish to use them.

They were grinning to each other as they came near and I could see they were more excited and nervous than they were angry or resolute. Seeing them made me feel old and weary with the weight of experience beyond theirs.

They drew rein in a line facing me and sat for a moment in silence. I do not know but I imagine they were wondering what they should do now. They probably expected to find the sheep tended by a meek and humble man whom they could torment while they made sport of destroying his woollies. What they faced was a man with a gun as large as theirs, and I am neither meek nor humble.

They glanced among themselves until the center one of the three licked his lips and nudged his mount a hesitant step forward.

"This is cattle country, mister," he said too loudly. "No sheep allowed."

"It's open season on the bastards around here," said the boy to his right. The first pulled his mouth into a hard, frowning line and nodded. They would soon be ready to commit themselves.

"Then I guess I'll just have to move my sheep along, won't I, boys?" I said. It did not satisfy them, as I was afraid it would not.

"Are you saying you're gonna run, sheepherder?" the second one accused with a sneer creeping onto his features. No doubt he had heard too much about gutless sheepherders.

"You saw us in plenty of time," the third cowboy observed in a normal tone of voice. "You had plenty of time to move away, and that's a good horse you're riding."

I smiled at him. "It's kind of difficult to herd sheep from three hills away, son. And they need closer tending than your bovines."

"Not these ones. Not anymore," the spokesman said.

The second boy edged his horse out to the side and forward a few feet and nodded toward my boots. "Looka there, Ralph. This sheepherder," he made the word sound like a curse word, "has him some boots just like a regular person. That don't seem right."

Ralph grinned, his confidence fed by the support of his friend. "I always heard sheepherders only wore one spur, too." He looked at me and asked, "How come you're dressed like a white man?"

I returned his smirk with my mildest grin. "My friends who wear just the one spur tell me if you get the first half of your horse to running the other half comes along with it, but it feels unbalanced to me to do it that way." To the third boy, who seemed the most sensible of them, I said, "It's been nice visiting with you boys, but I have work to do. If we stay here jawing at one another it could lead to hard feelings, and I don't hardly feel like a quarrel today. Whyn't you fellas drop this before it gets serious?"

The second boy worked himself into an anger over that. His face flushed red and he began to curse.

"We came here to kill us some sheep," the center one, Ralph, declared.

"An' you too if you don't stand aside," the second one shouted.

I sighed and checked to see where Beggar had positioned himself and worked very hard to keep my voice calm and mild. "Son, it just isn't in me to take water from anybody, even from a boy too young to know better, but I'll ask you kindly to ride away. It's my job to protect and tend these woollies, and do it I will. If you pull iron, boy, you'll need to turn it my way first."

Well, I guess that was a wrong thing to say because immediately that second boy's eyes lighted up until he was near to throwing sparks. He began hollering cuss words louder and louder and his excitement must have leaked through his knees to his horse for it started to prance and bob its head and its nostrils flared wide.

Ralph was getting pretty worked up by it all too, and he began yelling how they were going to kill every damned sheep I had and any more that might come onto this cow range. Even the third boy seemed to be getting agitated. He was swallowing often and blinking his eyes and clenching and reclenching his right hand into a fist. Their horses began to jigger and dance until the dust started to rise, and it was no trick to see they were working themselves up to it.

There wasn't much I could do without stepping aside and letting them gun the sheep but I figured I had to try. I could see in their eyes that this whole thing was still a lark to them and slightly unreal so that they would be thinking—and, no, that isn't right, for they would be feeling but not thinking now—they would be feeling that this was sport and so no real harm could come to them.

I stood in my stirrups and as loud and as sharp as I could I shouted, "*Quiet!*" and the sound of it cut through their yammer and stilled them until all of a sudden there was only the sound of their saddle leather shifting and behind me the low bleating of the wethers.

"I don't want to hurt you boys," I told them while I could, "but I'll not die myself to save your hides. Maybe you've never killed men before. I have. I don't like it, boys. It's an unpretty thing. Now ride away before I must do it again. Do you hear me, boys? If you don't back off I'll blow bloody holes in your bodies, and you'll foul the ground with your bleeding and somewhere there will be people in sorrow. Now ride away before this happens. Please!"

And I meant it and hoped without believing it that they would.

It was the second boy that turned ugly again and began to curse about sheep and sheepherders and to threaten what they were going to do to both. They built themselves back up toward it and there was no argument I could have made that would have helped. I sat on the blue horse and waited without listening to the words that were said but only to the rising pitch of their sound until the last of the blaspheming and the threatening were done and the second boy pulled his gun and had the others pull theirs.

Even then they did not believe harm could come to them and I waited until the second boy cocked his revolver and leveled it toward my flock while the other two pointed guns at me and finally, knowing I could not stop them otherwise, I palmed my old revolver and blew the second boy out of his saddle and then Ralph too.

Their horses bolted away riderless and the two boys died in the dust with bright blood frothing in the holes in their chests, and I called Beggar off the third youngster before he was finished.

The big dog had come up over the rump of the cowboy's horse and taken the boy in the back of the neck and carried him to the ground, and the boy was lucky enough to jam his arm between Beggar's jaws when the dog tried to shift toward a hold in his throat and so the boy was still alive.

I stepped down off the blue horse and called Beggar to my side and had him sit, trembling and eager to fight again, while I holstered my gun and went to see to this boy who now would know the difference between sport and blood. I still felt very old and very weary.

CHAPTER 6

The boy would be all right. He was rolled over on his side vomiting, but I do not believe the reaction had much to do with his own hurts. He had seen his friends and come face-on with the knowledge that death was something that could reach him too, and the first knowing of that can be a hard thing. I do not believe a boy can truly become a man until he learns that living is a short-term gift and not an endless right, and when I spoke to this cowboy now it would be to a different person from the one I'd been facing a few minutes before. I rolled him face down and unknotted his bandanna to use on the gashes Beggar had put in him.

"Lie still, boy. Bites are messy but they look worse than they really are."

"I'm not dying?" He swiveled his head to look at me and his eyes came back from some far place to find their focus on me. "You aren't going to kill me?"

"No, boy, I'll not hurt you. Let me tie this in place and I'll take a look at your arm. There. That bleeding will stop soon. Now help me roll you over. Good."

The puncture wounds on his forearm were not as ugly to look at but were the more dangerous. A bite like that can fester with poison while the flowing blood of the open gashes seems to clean those wounds. "I'll be right back," I told him and went to my packs for a flask of whiskey.

"Will this hurt?" he asked when I was ready to pour, but then he glanced toward the bodies of his two friends and clamped his mouth shut.

"It sure will," I said. "Go ahead and holler if you want." But I was betting he would not make a sound after the reminder he'd just given himself, and he did not although he went white and broke out in cold sweat against pale skin. "What's your name, boy?" I asked to take his mind from it.

"Billy. Billy Wendt." He said it through gritted teeth.

"All right, Billy Wendt. You're doing fine." I wrapped my own bandanna around his arm and checked the back of his neck. That had already just about quit bleeding. "You can call me Jude, by the way." I laid him back down and got my shovel off the packs so I could do the burying that needed done. I sent Beggar out to keep an eye on the sheep. They were starting to spread into a comfortable grazing pattern.

When I was done with that chore I put their guns and money and the few other things from their pockets into a spare sack for Billy Wendt to carry back to their folks if he knew where to find them.

"You can put markers over them later," I told Wendt. He'd been watching without saying anything while I worked. "I don't have any wood to carve for them. Anyway I don't know who they were."

He nodded.

"I suppose somebody will be along soon to fetch you back to your headquarters. Your horses took off toward the east."

Wendt shook his head. "We've been working out of a cow camp. Just the three of us. The outfit's owned by Mr. Pierson down in Cheyenne."

I sighed, though I really would have preferred to cuss. This boy couldn't be left alone. Not until I knew whether Beggar's toothmarks were going to putrefy. If they did he would be in no shape to tend himself and he'd be sure to die.

"Well," I said, "I got no spare saddle out here, but I expect you can get along without one if you have to. And I guess you have to. How far is it?"

"Less than an hour at an easy lope. An' I can manage it all right."

I laughed at him. "For somebody who was so het up about my sheep you sure forgot them easily. We'll start now, Billy Wendt, and if we're lucky we'll make it to your place before nightfall."

He looked toward the flock and toward the two fresh graves but he didn't say anything. I whistled to Beggar and signaled him to bunch the flock, then helped Wendt to his feet.

Before those cowboys found us the idea of wandering slowly across this beautiful grassland made me happy as a dead pig in the sunshine. Now, in Billy Wendt's tight-lipped company, the beauty of the day and the feeling of loose and easy freedom were gone.

It was not that the injured cowboy was being surly or unpleasant. Especially when you consider that he would've been grieving for the sudden loss of his friends, I would have to say that he was being pretty decent. It was only natural that he would want to be quiet for a time, and he did not look or act like he felt bitter toward me. He neither said nor implied any accusation.

I guess it was just that his presence—and the knowledge of those two unmarked graves behind us—sapped the pleasure from the day for me.

The afternoon wore slowly and for a change I felt, although I tried to conceal it, an impatience with the pace the wethers confined us to. I was glad when after nearly four hours Wendt said the cow camp was over the next rise.

The place was hardly imposing but it was nicely situated. A small creek ran here between two long folds in the ground. There was a good bit of brush along the water and some young trees. It looked like any older trees had been cut to build the camp or to supply firewood.

A log-fronted dugout with a pole and sod roof supplied living quarters, and more poles had been used to enclose a couple acres of corral for the string of horses. All three of the animals Wendt and his friends had been riding were grazing near the creek in sight of the corral. One of them seemed to have kicked or rolled its saddle loose but the others appeared to have their gear still intact.

"I'll bring your horses in as soon as I get you and the sheep settled," I said.

"All right, I . . . look . . . just downstream there's a nice open area the other side of that brush where there seems to be some water seepage in the ground. Good grass, anyway. You can, uh, put your sheep over there. Okay?"

"Sure. You go ahead and drop off here. I'll be along directly."

He looked surprised. "You'd trust me to go in alone? There's a couple guns in there."

"Billy Wendt, you don't much look like a murderer to me. If you show me I'm wrong, of course, I'll try to deal with it. Until then I figure it could get awful uncomfortable with us afraid to turn our backs on each other." I chirped to Beggar and he helped me drive the flock across the stream and turn them down toward the green flat. The boy had been right about the grass there, and with the water right beside them the woollies should have sheer comfort for several days. I left Beggar to keep an eye on them and went back to the camp.

"I hung those saddles on the fence," I told Wendt when I was inside, "and turned the horses into the pen."

He nodded and went on with stirring something in a pan on the folding sheet-metal stove they had in the dugout. That kind of stove is generally called a sheepherder's stove but this did not seem a good time to be making any jokes about that.

Other than the stove the dugout was pretty well free of modern conveniences. They had some stools and a rickety-wobbly table, all of them home cobbled from split logs, and that was about it. They were using sacks hung from pegs for storage instead of going to the bother of building shelves, and the bed arrangement seemed to be a free choice of floor space on which to spread your bedroll. There wasn't anything as fancy as a bunk or cot. Not much more had been done to provide lighting. The door could be left open during the daytime, of course, and there was a nub of candle tacked onto the tabletop with its own melted wax. Wood for the stove was just tossed onto the dirt floor, where it would be the handiest. The place had a close, damp, sour smell about it, a smell of earth and unwashed men. It also smelled as if someone had not always bothered to step outside for middle-of-the-night relief.

"You can put your bedroll anywhere you want," Wendt said. "I generally spread mine in that corner back there."

"Thanks, but I'll need to stay with the flock in case there's any coyotes about." The truth was that Beggar could take care of any coyote or any pack of them that came near. I just didn't want to be bedding down in a place that smelled as bad as this one did.

Wendt nodded and made no pretense of being disappointed he would not have my company. And of course I had done damned little to endear myself to him after I shot his two friends.

"You'll be leaving in the morning?" he asked.

"That kinda depends," I told him. "You'll likely be stiffened up and hurting pretty good by then. I doubt you'll be doing any riding for a day or two, and if that arm should start to turn green you'll have to have help."

"Why would you do that for me?"

"Boy, you might not of noticed it but I haven't yet offered hurt to anyone without it was pushed onto me. Well, I don't figure to start now either, Billy Wendt. You see, I get into a town from time to time. When I do I generally take a hired room. And sometimes those places have mirrors in them for shaving. I kinda like to be able to look myself in the eye when that happens."

Billy Wendt clouded up and acted as if he'd like to get mad. "They weren't going to hurt you, you know. They were just going to have some fun and keep those damn sheep off our grass."

"Son, if you can seriously stand there and tell me you'd sit quiet and watch somebody shoot Mr. Pearce's beeves, I will understand that comment better. I won't respect you worth a damn, but I will be more understanding about it."

He dropped his eyes and stuck his lower lip out. "Pierson. They're Mr. Pierson's cows. Anyway you didn't have to kill them. They were out for a good time, that's all. You could've just wounded them or something."

"Guns make lousy playtoys, Billy Wendt, and sensible people tend to take them real serious. And I think you've heard too much and seen too little about the use of them in a fight. Anybody who tells you he's good enough to shoot for an arm or something in the middle of a three-on-one fight has got to be lying to you, boy. Nobody is that good. Not even me."

He looked angrier than ever and it seemed clear he had decided I wasn't going to murder him in his own camp. "You talk awful big. You must think you're a real he-wolf with the run of the hills."

"I'm still alive."

He slammed his spoon down and winced at the pain brought on by the quick motion but he snapped, "You do just fine facing a couple cowboys who've never been in a fight before. Maybe you won't do so good when the Association hears about you." Defiantly he added, "Or are you gonna murder me now to keep me from telling them? That's the only way to shut me up, mister. The only way in the whole damned world."

He looked just as feisty as a cur pup standing there with his jaw stuck out, and I could not help but laugh at the picture he presented. If that arm didn't fester young Billy Wendt was going to be just fine.

"Do your goodest, Billy," I told him with a grin. "As long as you tell them true I'll not hold a thing against you. Now if you will excuse me, I have to go look after my sheep." I touched my hat brim to him and chuckled my way out of there.

CHAPTER 7

I stayed four days there, near if not exactly with Billy Wendt and his cow camp, and at the end of that time the soreness was beginning to leave his neck and I was pleased to see there were no red halos of infection around the punctures in his arm. I saddled a horse for him before I left and he gave me a dire warning that he would use it to ride for the nearest Association man, and he probably didn't believe me when I wished him well. But I did.

Brock or someone like him would find me sooner or later anyhow and if it made Wendt happy to make it the sooner, well, that would be all right by me. I figured the nearest sure way to reach the Association would be in Cheyenne. A strong man with a relay of horses or with one really good one could make that distance in less than a day despite the length of time I'd been trailing my sheep north from there. In Wendt's condition I guessed he would reach the city sometime the next day. Which meant I probably had a couple days of peace and quiet I could enjoy. More if they didn't happen to find me. Which made for a fun kind of problem.

It should be no great secret by now that I was heading for the northeastern part of the territory. The clever thing to do, then, would be to turn south instead of north, swing east into Nebraska or Dakota, whichever one happened to be across the line from here, and I really wasn't sure which it would be, and then drive on north outside the Association's domain.

Ah, but Richard Brock knew I enjoyed playing guessing games with him, and he was a suspicious fellow as I could well remember. I might just count on him anticipating a jump across the territorial border and choose instead to move west into the empty grass and lose myself and my flock out there.

I thought about that a bit and then did some laughing for Beggar's benefit and my own and let the wethers lay as plain a trail as possible due north. After a while I drifted them into thicker grass where they should pass without a trace.

You know, it is a funny thing but there seem to be an awful lot of city fellas who believe a man, especially an Indian, can learn to track until he almost seems to be magic about it. The plain truth is that tracking is mostly guesswork, figuring what the quarry is likely to do next and then trying to confirm it by some sort of physical sign. And while there is a lot a knowing man can read from tracks, there first has to be some track for him to read. Sand or mud or soft earth you can read like a book. Rock is apt to be scratched by iron shoes. But grass . . . that just swallows the tracks of whatever walks across it unless it is trampled by animal after animal enough to beat down a path. So as soon as I figured we'd left enough of a "false" trail to convince Brock we weren't really headed north I just spread the sheep wide and kept on going north. I was kind of looking forward to telling Brock about it later. Assuming it worked.

And it sure seemed to, for we spent the next couple weeks without laying eyes on another human being.

It was a pleasant time, and I enjoyed it. I've never been much for advertising my whereabouts with a night-burning fire, but after I had the sheep settled and supper out of the way old Beggar would come in and settle himself against my leg for some ear scratching and I could read if there was still a little light in the sky or just sit and enjoy a pipeful of tobacco and the clean scent of moving air. It was never too long before I dozed off and whenever I did I knew Beggar would ease away and keep an eye on things. Both of us would waken every so often through the night to raise a head and make sure things were well with the flock. When there were no coyotes or wolves near, Beggar would curl close and warm my side and the movement of one would usually rouse the other so both knew the other was on the job.

Like I said, it was a pleasant time, and I enjoyed it thoroughly.

Eventually we got where we were going and to tell the truth, for a time there that afternoon I just sat on a hilltop and marveled.

We were at the edge of the Black Hills and whatever it was I had expected from the name Black Hills has been wiped from my mind now by the beauty of their reality. I suppose I must have been expecting something like the mesas of the Southwest with maybe some crossbreeding to the foothills of the mountains with the green and gray of forest and rock up high and the bleak bareness of arid scrub below. I don't honestly remember now, but I know I was not prepared for what I found here.

When I topped that Wyoming hill and saw what was spread before me I simply had to step down off the sorrel and sit for a while just to look.

There was some cloud rolling in, low and white and touched with steely gray, with sunlight streaming out of patches of blue to make a shifting pattern of light and shadow across the ground.

The land here was still that rich, rolling carpet of sweet grass but rising out of it now were, quite literally, black hills. Huge loaves of high ground made black with thickly forested slopes that had to mean available water was there as well. It was the most perfect land I had ever seen, wide and beautiful and empty, and I sat nearly an hour looking at it before I moved to take Howard Blackburn's sheep down on the grass leading into it.

I drove the wethers another day before I found a road and enough signs of civilization to decide I had arrived at the place where these woollies would grow and fatten. I needed to be close enough to people that I could resupply without leaving the sheep long, even if this meant I had to crowd the local cattlemen some.

The grass was far from being overgrazed here, maybe because of good management but more likely because of the terrible winter die-up so recently. That storm had ruined a good many cattlemen and left the door open to sheep when so many of the northern and plains beeves were killed off, and it was no doubt one of the reasons why Blackburn and men like him were making the attempt now to bring woollies in where only cattle had been before.

Anyway, I chose a fairly isolated stretch of grass between two towering hills. The flat where I placed my flock was not more than seven miles long and a couple wide but the grass was good and several springs rose at the base of the easternmost hill to form a thin creek. There was a rocky, steep-walled fold in the flank of the other hill where the sheep could be put for close protection if need be, although there was no water there and little graze. Altogether it was a good spot and I set up a more or less permanent camp near one of the springs and hung my provisions and gear in one of whatever kind of needled tree it was that covered the slopes. Here I would stay a while.

Next morning I saddled the blue horse and watered the sheep and took them to the north end of my little flat. I let them spread out there and left them under Beggar's care while I took a scout around.

It had been my intention to circle this east hill first and the western one the next day. Each figured to be a ride of twenty miles more or less and without the encumbrance of slow-walking sheep it would take little time at a steady lope-and-jog traveling pattern and would not leave the sheep untended too long.

My plan washed out that first morning.

The other side of the hill—which was big enough that it would have been called a mountain anywhere else—looked over a much broader grass flat to a much larger hill, or mountain, maybe eight or ten miles distant. The flat between was more of that beautiful rolling grass and was dotted with a herd of sleek, heavy-bodied beeves that showed some upgrading from their Texas range-cow ancestry. I saw a few blocky-bodied, beefy-looking bulls that seemed to be crossbreeds themselves but that had short horns and a lot of deep red in their coats.

The scar of a wagon road cut across the grass from north to south, curving off to the east before it was lost to view. A spur off the road led toward the east side of the hill I was already coming to think of as my own. I tucked the blue roan in closer to the rocky outcroppings at the base of the hill and slowed him to a walk.

Set there in the shelter of the hill where it would catch the early-morning sun was one of the prettiest little ranch setups I have ever seen.

It was neither grand nor grandiose but rather was snug and . . . neat somehow, almost tidy in appearance.

The house was no crude dugout but was built solidly of squared and fitted logs. It was low-roofed and long enough that it had to contain several rooms, and it had glazed windows and a sturdy little roof over the front stoop.

A low-roofed barn had been built with nearly as much care and the outbuildings were sheathed with split logs. A series of pens and corrals had been built below the barn, each of them with heavy posts and short, straight poles. Someone had gone to considerable trouble in selecting and cutting each of those pieces of wood, and each of them had been peeled.

A garden plot had been laid out northeast of the house—the barn was just south of it—and a bed of turned earth right along the front of the house held some low shrubs and some greenery that I would have bet carried flowers at some time of the year. Whoever lived here had come to stay.

I had mixed emotions about seeing such a place here. On the one hand I kind of admired and would not have minded meeting the man who would make such a place for himself. On the other I was not altogether that keen on the idea of having a cowman for such a close neighbor. If he didn't go to the gun himself right away when he saw my sheep he would certainly make a good tool for the Association when they started their maneuvering to get rid of me.

I was undecided at first about whether I should make myself known here—it would tip him to me, but an honest man generally finds it harder to go to war with someone he's jawed with than with a stranger—and what decided me was some movement I saw down around the garden. There were some chickens there on the prowl for bugs.

Now I am no great trencherman and don't too much care what goes onto the table so long as it does the job. But if there is one thing I do love and do miss when I'm out away from folks it is an egg. Lordy, but I do love an egg, any way it can be fixed, for there isn't a bad way. If these people had chickens—and they did—I was sure going to call on them. I commenced to grinning and bumped that roan horse forward.

I took him into the yard at a jog, turning to rubberneck at those black-and-white speckled chickens as I went by the garden.

Like a fool I was turned around in the saddle admiring them when I heard the slam of a door and the even more distinctive sound that I had heard too often before. Someone threw the lever of a rifle and jacked a cartridge into place. I did cuss myself a bit before I reined in the blue horse and turned to look.

CHAPTER 8

It was a woman standing there behind that rifle and that made me even more nervous than I might have been. A woman is apt to get fidgety and scared and might shoot when she didn't have need to. I put on my very best and most charming smile and tried to look just as inoffensive as ever anyone could.

"Good morning to you, ma'am," I said and reached real slow to touch the brim of my hat. "I think one of us is making a bit of a mistake here. Should I take it you'd like me to leave?"

"You can take it I want to know your business here," she said.

I reached an arm back to point without taking my eyes off her. "It's about those chickens, ma'am. I was hopeful you might have a few eggs to sell." I grinned at her. "I have this terrible weakness for eggs, you see, and they can be awful seldom for a wandering man."

She gave a snort like she didn't even half believe me and said, "You can do better than that, surely."

I spread my hands wide and innocent and told her, "Lady, if I'd come in here fixing to tell you a tall one, I will admit that I would've had a real good story prepared. But the fact is that I just happened to notice those hens an' thought they might've left some spare fruit around. Now if you'd rather, I can turn right around an' never bother you again. Just back off of that trigger a little and I will."

The muzzle of the rifle was starting to waver as if the rifle—and it wasn't any light saddle carbine, I could see, but a heavy-barreled rifle in one of the bigger calibers—was beginning to be too much for her to hold steady. Her expression became less and less certain and finally she exhaled with a big sigh and let the muzzle sag the rest of the way down. I think we both felt better after she did. "You can step down if you want," she said.

"Thank you, ma'am." I touched the brim of my hat to her and got off and led the blue horse forward.

"I could spare you a sack of eggs," she said. She grimaced and added, "There isn't much I have extra of, but at least I have eggs."

Now that I could see the woman instead of just that open muzzle I could see she was taller and maybe a few years older than I'd thought at first. She was awfully thin, which made her seem smaller than she was, and had enough crow's feet and what people like to call laugh wrinkles to suggest she was coming near to thirty if she wasn't there yet, though she probably was. But from the look in her eyes and the bitterness in her voice I didn't think she had been doing much laughing of late.

Her hair was cropped fairly short as if she didn't want to be bothered with tending it although it was clean and brushed but not curled or put into a bun. It was brown in color and her eyes were of an almost greenish cast.

Properly speaking she was not what you would consider to be an exceptionally handsome woman, but there was something about her, an air about her or maybe just a feeling around her, that kept the attention coming back and focusing on her until you got the impression that this rather plain, middlin'-tall female person just might be a whole lot of woman. She did not seem to be particularly conscious of this effect she had or maybe it was just that she had been aware of it so long and had come to terms with it so long before that she no longer bothered to give it thought. Whatever, I kept on looking at her where normally I would not have paid so much attention to another man's woman.

The moment of inspection stretched beyond what should be considered proper and I thought I could see a hint of wry amusement in those green eyes before she said, "I believe it was eggs you wanted, mister . . . ?"

"Yes, ma'am." I swept my hat off, feeling for some reason like a schoolboy caught with his ink jar uncapped and the end of a pigtail between his fingers. "The name is Priest, ma'am. Jude for short."

"All right, Jude." She cocked her head and gave me a speculative kind of look that seemed to last longer than it really did. "You can tie your horse over there if you like. And I believe it is close enough to dinnertime that you might want to join me. I can fix some of those surplus eggs."

"That's awfully kind of you, ma'am," I said but she had already turned to go inside.

I tied the horse where she had indicated and spotted a wash-stand a few feet beyond the hitch rail. Someone had walled up a little spring with mortared rock. An overflow pipe and an open ditch fed a trickle of water toward the stock pens, and a gate arrangement had been built to divert the water to the garden when it was wanted there. An enameled washbasin was on the stand beside the wall along with a covered pan of soft soap. I used the soap liberally since I got so little chance to and flapped my hands in the air to dry them. There was no towel on the little hook screwed into the side of the wooden stand.

Feeling a lot better then, I went back to the front of the house and made some noise stamping the dirt from my boots.

"Come on in," she called through the screen door, which was a refinement you wouldn't normally find, at least not in the part of the country I came from.

The inside of the place was fairly plain but very neat and very clean. A puncheon floor had been smoothed and soaped until it was nearly white around the scattering of many-colored rag rugs. The furniture was made of wood, shaped and fitted by someone who knew what he was doing and took his time to do it well. Everything —table and chairs, armchairs, wall shelves, mantelpiece, cupboards and massive sideboard—had been stoned and rubbed to a satin gloss. Even the walls had been stoned and either oiled or waxed.

The large main room had a fireplace in the back wall right in the center. To the right of that was the kitchen part of the room with the big table and an iron cooking range. To the left was the sitting area with a pair of easy chairs covered with buffalo robes, and some shelves filled with knickknacks and porcelain pretties and, most of all, with books.

The woman was whipping something in a bowl and had a pile of broken eggshells beside her. A coffee pot on the stove had not yet started to boil so I guessed she was not expecting her man home at midday or she would already have had coffee made and ready.

"This won't take long," she said.

"All right." I hung my hat on a peg by the door and realized with something of a shock that I had almost reached as well to un-buckle my gunbelt. It had been years since I had felt an impulse like that and even longer since I'd actually done it. It was a surpris-

ing thing to feel again now and, disturbed, I turned away from the
woman and walked to the shelves holding the books.

The names on the much-worn cloth and leather-covered spines
included a number of the dead poets whom I considered to be old
friends but were long on titles that were new to me, most of them
having Greek-sounding names. Most of the volumes were quite
small and all of them had received a great deal of handling. I
turned to look at the woman again.

"I don't suppose you and the mister would consider doing some
trading, ma'am?" I asked hopefully.

"Trading what?" she asked, and I hooked a thumb over my
shoulder toward the books. She smiled and shook her head.

I shrugged and grinned. "I had to try, anyway. A man traveling
light and long can't carry much with him and doesn't pass up whatever chances he gets."

"I wish I could part with some of them, but . . ." And I understood that she could not. "You can come to the table now if you
wish, Mr. Priest."

The meal was a good one and was eaten in a silence that was neither awkward nor uncomfortable. When it was done I carried
water in and found a fresh cup of coffee at my place when I returned.

"You would oblige me if you would wait until I have finished the
washing, Mr. Priest," she said quite formally so I replaced my hat
on the peg and sat to wait. When she was finished with the dishes
she refilled my cup and brought her own to the table. She sat opposite me and gave me a long stare with those green eyes. "I take it
that you are not employed by Lawrence Greenough, Mr. Priest?"

I shook my head.

"And you have had experience handling cows?"

"Yes, ma'am."

"Then I would like to offer you a job." Just like that, flat and
blunt and no beating around the bush.

"I'm sorry, ma'am. I'm not looking for work right now."

A look of annoyance passed across her face and she nibbled at
her lower lip for a moment. Resolutely she went on. "I do not know
what you may have heard about me, Mr. Priest, but you look like
an honest man and one not easily frightened. I wish you would at
least consider my offer." She would have said more but I held up a
hand to stop her.

"I guess I didn't make myself clear, ma'am. First, I don't know anything at all about either you or anyone named Greenough. I've never been in this country before and haven't spoken to a living soul since I got here. Second, the reason I couldn't consider accepting a job is that I already have one. I'm here in my employer's interests, not my own."

I thought that would make everything nice and plain so that I could pay for my meal and be on my way in comfort, but the woman's face kind of crumpled and for an instant there was a deep pain lying there in the green of her eyes. She gained control of herself quickly and gave me a bitter, phony smile and said, "Well, that is that then, isn't it. Thank you anyway, Mr. Priest. Good day to you."

I started to rise and leave, and perhaps I should have. Instead I peered for a moment into the dregs of the coffee left in my cup and then said, "Perhaps you might want to tell me about it . . . ?"

She fidgeted for a moment, toying with her fingers on the table surface, but before she spoke she looked up at me boldly and with no appeal for sympathy in either voice or expression.

"My husband was one of the first to bring cattle into this country, Mr. Priest. He certainly was the first to come here with the idea of making a permanent home here rather than exploiting the land for quick profits and free grass. He had a dream, and he built carefully toward that end. He believed in selective breeding and close management, and he did fairly well here.

"He was never a large-scale rancher and was always regarded by the larger owners as one of the small-time interlopers, but our profits were satisfactory and were growing. When the hard winter came and the die-up ruined or at least crippled so many of the large ranchers, back warm and comfortable themselves in Cheyenne or Chicago or wherever, John was out there with his animals chopping ice to keep the water open and feeding hay he had stored against just such need. He was able to winter over nearly all of our stock. I don't think we lost a dozen animals, and they were the oldest and the most feeble of the herd.

"Lawrence Greenough is one of the large ranchers. He is a greedy man and a jealous one. He could not believe that our cattle could have survived where his died." She snorted. "Enough of his drank at holes John kept open and ate hay that John had cut. Even so, Greenough's book count said he should have more cattle than he did. You know about book counting?"

I nodded. Many men, including not a few who should know better, did not count their cows but tallied only their calves and then multiplied by five to give them a count on how many animals they were supposed to own. There were even those foolish enough to buy herds on the basis of such counting.

"Anyway, last year Greenough accused John of stealing from him. Anyone could plainly see the difference between our breeding and his, but Greenough muddied the water enough to have John removed from the Cattlemen's Association. And of course that meant that we could not participate in the Association-controlled roundups. I never will know how many of our calves Greenough was able to steal that way, but I know there were enough of them to really hurt.

"John took what he could salvage and drove them south. He never came back, and the stock inspector swears none of our cattle were shipped from any point in Wyoming *or* Nebraska *or* South Dakota. People in Cheyenne won't look into any of it. They just snicker and imply that John got fed up and ran." Her eyes flashed defiance.

"He would have done no such thing. This was where he intended to stay to the end of his days, and I believe that he did exactly that, no matter what anyone says." The spark of anger faded.

"Since then I haven't been able to hire hands and of course I can't be part of the Association roundups. I have . . . well dammit I'm nearly broke. I was hoping you would work my cattle on shares. It seems you cannot do that. And I apologize for taking up so much of your time."

I took a deep breath and stared into the bottom of my coffee cup some more. The temptation was strong to assure her that everything would be well. But that would have been a very foolish thing to do. What possible words of comfort could I have offered her that would not have been empty ones?

CHAPTER 9

The woman wouldn't accept payment for the meal, but she did sell me some more eggs to carry along with me. She fixed them up in a cloth sack with dried grass for padding, and I tied them to my saddle and rode away from there after telling her no more than that I would be in the area for a while and would stop by again if she didn't mind. She said she did not.

It was only later that I realized I did not know her name. As well as I could remember she had never mentioned it. That her husband's name had been—or still was—John was all I knew.

Nor did I know why I was bothering to concern myself with thinking about such a thing as a woman's name when there were so many important things I could have worried about. I mean, she was not even all that attractive a woman. Certainly she would never be called beautiful. Yet there was something about her, something both strong and sensuous that commanded attention and reached out to keep dragging my thoughts back to her. I did not want to have my thoughts captured by a woman, especially by one who did not know herself if she was a wife or a widow, but I seemed to have little choice in the matter and it annoyed me.

I pushed the blue horse too hard and paid too little attention to the land as I completed the circuit around the loaf-shaped hill that sheltered Howard Blackburn's wethers, but I got back to them well before dark.

Beggar rushed in ear-flopping bounds to greet me as I came near, and if he had had any trouble with predators while I was away I could find no sign of it.

I got down to scratch him and for a time he abandoned his dignity to roll on his back like a pup so I could reach his belly and make him squirm in the ecstasy of the attention.

The roan was sweating heavily after the ride so I gave him a good rubdown and switched my saddle to the sorrel horse before I gathered the sheep and moved them closer to my camp for the night.

I ate early and sat in the gathering dusk with Beggar curled beside my leg and the coffee pot close to hand. I found myself thinking without reason that it would be darker on the other side of the tall hill where light from the western sky would be blocked. This seemed to be my day for extraneous thoughts.

Evening brought out the yapping of coyotes somewhere near, but I heard no wolf song and that pleased me. I had no way of knowing yet if there were any big cats in the area. There would almost certainly be some of the smaller cats here but they will seldom try to take prey as large as a half-grown wether. And if they did Beggar could deal with them. He might need help with a lion or a wolf pack but with nothing smaller.

Once the fire had died away and full dark had fallen I smoked a last pipe of tobacco and spread my bedroll. It always takes me a few minutes to get everything just right for my sleeping, but I have gotten set in my ways and don't think I could be comfortable if everything wasn't just where it ought to be. My gunbelt has to be beside my head and my night gun along my right leg. I carry a good rifle on my saddle, of course, but a rifle is poor help at night and so I pack a short-barreled shotgun and a little buckshot for use on anything that comes prowling after dark. Mostly, though, I depend on Beggar after dark.

My sleep was light and not overly restful that night and come morning I found myself thinking that while my camp was still in shadow under a bright sky, the other side of the hill would be taking a bath in yellow light.

I was sitting there thinking things like that and kind of wondering what the woman's name was when Beggar's head came up and he shifted his legs tighter under him. "Good boy," I said and waited.

A moment later I could see the horse and rider coming along the base of the hill from the south. I took a second look to make sure and then rummaged in my gear to find my spare cup, which I filled and placed on the ground on the other side of the fire.

A minute or two later the man dismounted and tied his horse to a low-growing tree before he walked over to join me.

"Good morning, Richard." I pointed to the coffee and he squatted beside it.

"That was a helluva trick to play on a man," he said.

I grinned. "Which one?"

"I caught hell for that, Jude. Right through downtown, for God's sake. You didn't have to do that. Do you have any notion how mad you made those people?"

"Considerable, I'll bet. To tell you the truth I was wondering if it would be you I'd see up here. Hope they didn't take it all out on you when you got off that train."

Brock shook his head and wiped some imaginary sweat off his brow. "It almost wasn't me staying on this one. If there'd been anyone else available there probably would've been someone else here now."

"I thought you boys came in flocks. Like sheep. Why, to hear the sheepmen tell it, half the population of the territory is made up of Association guns looking for someone to shoot. The other half, of course, being the Association men they work for."

He pulled at his chin and snorted. "A couple years ago they wouldn't have been all that wrong either. In case you haven't heard, though, things are tough these days for the cowmen. There aren't so many members as there used to be and the ones still on the rolls aren't so rich as they were either." He smiled. "They tell me things will get better again if the range management division can keep the grass from being ruined." He turned his head to eye the wethers milling around at the edge of the water.

"Isn't it funny how opinions will differ? I've heard it said that in a few years your bosses will be running sheep of their own."

"Yeah, well . . ."

"In the meantime we'll poke along and do our best, you and me," I said. "How do you figure to approach this, anyway?" I asked him point blank. "You obviously don't figure to pull out your gun and start destroying sheep right away."

Brock grimaced. "No. I heard some youngsters down South already tried that."

"They wouldn't have it any other way. Is there a warrant out?"

He thought about it for a minute and then apparently decided there would be no point in lying about it. A writ wasn't likely to scare me away. He shook his head. "No, the Wendt boy told them his buddies started it. He, uh, said they all three had their guns out before you pulled."

"Good. He seemed like a pretty decent kid, really."

"Yeah, well it didn't do him a whole lot of good. His boss decided the story could have been told a little different from what it was. He fired the kid and put him on the blacklist."

"I'm sorry to hear that, Richard," I said, and I was. I paused and added, "You people really do have a blacklist then. Hell, I thought that was just so much bull."

"No bull about it," Brock insisted. "They put it down in black and white and send it to every member and update it every so often. Once a fella's name hits that list he's through cowboying in this country for sure, and there's not too many other employers who want to antagonize the Association either. The blacklist generally means a man might as well move on, because he's through in Wyoming."

"You work for some hard people, Richard." I raised my eyebrows but if he got my meaning he ignored the question.

It was his business, of course, and I did not know all the facts. I knew the Association paid awfully well and maybe that was the full and final reason he worked for them. Maybe not. Certainly I had no special admiration for Howard Blackburn but I was drawing his pay. He gave me the chance to work out on my own. Maybe the Association gave Brock something he wanted besides money.

One thing, though. If I didn't especially like Blackburn I at least didn't talk him down to other people. I wondered if Brock's dressing down by the boys in Cheyenne had kinda put him off on his employers. If so that might be a useful thing, for it takes either a lot of loyalty or a lot of lawlessness to send a man into dishonest dealings on someone else's behalf.

Regardless of his reasons I figured I might as well take some advantage of Brock's talkative mood.

And while there were a whole bunch of things I could have prodded him on, when I opened my mouth what popped out was, "Do you know a fella called Lawrence Greenough?"

"Boy oh boy," Brock said. "And I thought you were supposed to be new to this country. Or did Blackburn fill you in? Yeah, I know Mr. Greenough, all right. And yeah, this is his little private empire you're trespassing on. Or it is to hear him tell it, anyhow."

"What's he like?"

Brock shrugged. "Rich, but not half as rich as he was nor a tenth as rich as he'd like to be. He got hurt in the die-up, though not as bad as some, and now he wants it all back and no waiting about it. I would say Mr. Greenough is a man with a great sense of the future and very little patience."

"Is he the one you'll be reporting to up here?"

Brock shook his head. "You wouldn't find him this far from the center of things. Not very often, you wouldn't. He lives in Cheyenne. Hangs around with the political crowd, especially the statehood bunch." I raised my eyebrows and got a grin in return. "There are some who figure they can't have but so much influence as long as the federal government has territorial control out here. They believe they'd have a freer hand with a state government controlled by beef interests. The other side sees it exactly the opposite. They figure they can hold the real power by way of getting their appointees in from a government a couple thousand miles away. Greenough happens to favor statehood, but both sides want the same end."

"Everybody wants to handle the reins," I said.

"That's about it." Brock shrugged. "I can't say that I blame them."

Maybe he didn't, but personally I wouldn't want to be saddled with someone else's problems. Nor jump in on someone else's good times either. I just wanted to be left alone in a country empty enough that I don't have to beg someone's pardon every time I pass wind.

"Greenough likes to do things inside the law then?" I asked.

Brock started to snort out a laugh at that but finally realized he was going too far with his talking out of school. He clomped his jaw shut and gave me a hard look before he said, "*All* of our members are law-abiding stockmen, and the Association works in full cooperation with local law-enforcement agencies, Priest."

"Uh huh," I said in a voice dry enough that I didn't think he could possibly mistake my disbelief of such a statement.

"You can think what you like," he said, "but when I get those sheep out of here—and you can believe that I *will* run them out—it will be by fair means."

I gave him a long, slow grin and said, "I notice, Richard, that you said you were gonna get the sheep out of here. You know, I hope, that I go with 'em. Or stay, as the case may be. It's kind of a package deal, my friend. And I do get stubborn at times."

Brock set his empty cup aside and from the look on his face I was wondering if he was wishing he'd slipped the thong off his hammer before he walked to my fire. "Don't threaten me, Priest."

"So who's threatening?" I asked innocently, my palms wide and a broad smile on my face.

Brock did not seem in a mood now to return the smile. He came to his feet in a fluid motion that reminded me once again that he looked like a quick and a competent fellow—although neither had yet been proven—and said, "Remember what I told you, Priest. I'll do it by fair means." He stabbed a finger in my direction. "But I will damned sure do it."

He spun on his heel and began stalking off toward his horse.

"You're welcome for the coffee," I called to his rapidly receding back.

I was feeling in a pretty good mood about the start of this day, even if I had done kind of a dumb thing. There Brock was, feeling as talkative as I was ever likely to find him, and instead of finding out what he intended to do about Howard Blackburn's woolly invasion I had gone and used up his mood asking him about Lawrence Greenough.

Oh well, I decided. It was Greenough who claimed private rights to this public grass. Maybe Blackburn's interests and the woman's were not completely dissimilar here. If they were, that was just too bad. I didn't really regret my moment of curiosity anyway.

I waited until Brock was out of sight and Beggar had settled back down at my side and then reached for the last splash of coffee in the pot. It was about time I did some work.

CHAPTER 10

Nothing much happened the rest of the day—which is just the way I like it—except for Beggar running a pair of coyotes and bringing down the female. She had been nursing, and I hoped the pups weren't old enough yet to get along without her. It would save some long-run trouble if they couldn't. I also had to fight off a temptation that day. I had to keep tending to business and make myself ignore a desire to go buy more eggs.

By evening, though, it was apparent that Richard Brock had been tending to his business too. A couple cowboys showed up at the north end of the grass flat. They sat their horses in plain sight and never offered to come near enough for a rifle shot, which I would not have taken even if they had moved in closer. I doubt that Brock really thought he could make me nervous just from having someone keep an eye on the flock but it was a fairly standard form of harassment and no harm in trying.

Late the next morning Brock returned with a pair of newcomers at his elbows. They weren't the same fellows who had been on parade the evening before, or at least one of them was not, as he was a lot beefier man than either of those riders had been.

I was in camp fixing to make myself a light lunch. They ignored the sheep and jangled right up to my fire with much noise from bit chains and loose-roweled spurs, enough of it that I wondered if I was supposed to remember that so I wouldn't think of them when someone slipped in quietly some night.

Since I didn't invite them down right away Brock nodded politely and stayed in his saddle.

"Hullo, Jude." He inclined his head toward the man on his left and said, "This is Sheriff Arlo Herring and his deputy, George Herring."

The names made them out to be kin of some sort, but you

couldn't tell it from looking at them. Nor would I have figured Arlo to be the head monkey.

Maybe it is just because folks tend to think of a bigger man as the authoritarian one in a crowd, but I think I would have guessed George to be the leader anyway. He was not only big—big but not fat—but also he was older and looked the smarter of the two. Neither of them had that belligerent, cock-of-the-walk smugness that so often goes along with a badge. Arlo looked downright ordinary, and it was plain that neither of them was much of a professional at enforcing laws. I would have bet that the election that put Arlo in office had been a family affair in a sparsely populated county. I began to wonder if they might be cowmen, perhaps Association members, who handled their lawing chores part-time.

Arlo cleared his throat pointedly and Brock said, "I happened to mention to the sheriff that you had moved, uh, livestock onto the range here, and he said there have been recent reports of stolen sheep in this area. I told him I was sure you wouldn't mind establishing yourself as an authorized agent here."

"I guess I can if I need to," I told him.

"Can we step down then?"

"I don't see why not."

They dismounted and stretched their legs like they'd been riding a while. George gathered all three sets of reins and led the horses away to water and tie them.

"I'll put some coffee on," I said, "but you'll either have to share a cup or provide your own. I don't have but two."

Arlo called to his deputy to bring cups from their saddlebags, and I carried my big camp pot to the spring to fill it. I've spent enough time in dry country that I have the habit of never setting up so close to water that my being there would frighten away any animals that might need to come to it during the night. This particular flat was too well watered for that to be a problem here but I could see no reason to make myself uncomfortable by violating a habit.

I put the water on to boil and set to begin cranking the little grinder to prepare the coffee. The others settled themselves on the ground nearby.

"You, uh, do have the necessary papers," Arlo said.

"Of course."

"And you would not mind producing them," he went on flatly.

"I'll be glad to show them to anyone with a valid need to see them," I said just as mild as could be.

"Fine." He seemed to think that was all settled then.

Me, I went right on grinding beans. When I figured I had enough I dumped them into the pot and sat back to wait for the water to reach a boil.

"Where are the papers?" Arlo asked after a little while.

"I keep them put up in a wallet," I told him truthfully. I decided the water had boiled long enough so I moved the pot off the fire and set it down to let the grounds settle.

Brock was beginning to look annoyed. "You don't have to make this difficult, you know."

I grinned at him. "Except for dying there isn't a whole lot that I *have* to do, Richard. And I'll put that off just as long as I can."

"You aren't being very funny, young man," Arlo said. He couldn't have been more than a few years older than me. "Now let me see those papers."

I sighed. "Mr. Herring, surely by now you've figured . . ."

"*Sheriff* Herring," George interrupted.

"Thank you. Mr. Herring, surely by now you've figured out that you are going to be caught in the middle of a fuss with the written law on one side and the interpreters of the law on another. However you might feel about it, there are going to be some real tough decisions to be made here. You might as well know right now that I'm going to expect you to take this letter by letter. As long as you can do that it can stay a problem of law instead of people."

"You think there's a difference?"

"Yes, sir, I do. Both sides really believe they are right here, so you have only the law to fall back on."

"Then why won't you show me those papers?"

"I never said I wouldn't, Mr. Herring," I held a hand up toward George before he could correct me again, "but take it by the book and do it right. Now then, you rode in here announced as the county sheriff but I never saw you before. Anybody could call himself that, to me or to Mr. Brock here. So far I haven't seen either a badge or a commission of office. Would you mind showing me one or the other of them?"

The sheriff nodded calmly enough, but George began to look angry. Well, that was one of the things I was trying to find out. Games are all right in their place but I don't generally play them just to aggravate people. I just figured it wouldn't hurt to know a little more about these people I might be dealing with in the near future. And George might look like the brighter of the two but he was also the easier prodded of them.

Arlo dipped two fingers into his vest pocket and pulled out a badge. He flipped it toward me. I plucked it out of the air and glanced at it—it was a cheap kind of shield that could have been ordered from any number of supply houses—and tossed it back to him. I rose and began pouring coffee.

"Thank you, sheriff. Since you say there have been reports of sheep thefts in the area I won't question where those woollies might've come from in this cow country, sir, and I won't ask to see any fliers or papers on that. Naturally I'll be glad to show you my papers."

None of the three of them flinched though we all knew there hadn't been any sheep around here to be stolen. Still, I was hoping the sheriff was honest enough that he disliked the idea of someone catching him in a lie. It might keep him a little straighter the next time.

I took the wallet from one of the pack sacks hung in a tree by the camp and shuffled through the wads of paper there. There seemed no point in allowing the sheriff to see all of them. I sorted out the ones that seemed appropriate and handed them to him.

Arlo pulled a small case from his breast pocket, took out a pair of spectacles and examined Blackburn's paperwork at length. As he finished with each sheet he handed it to George who read them more quickly and passed them on to Brock.

"All in order," Arlo said as he finished with the last of them. He handed it to George who gave it to Brock without bothering to look at it. "Sorry to have inconvenienced you, Mr. Priest."

"No trouble at all, sheriff. You'll find I'm a law-abiding sort. I have no objection to things being handled strict and true under the law."

He gave me a level gaze out of dark brown eyes and said, "I hope you mean that, Mr. Priest. If you do, we should have no quarrel."

"Oh, I do, sheriff. I don't expect to quarrel with any man unless he brings it to me first. And any time you need me, from now until I take these sheep out to market them, you'll be able to find me somewhere close around here."

Arlo removed his spectacles and tucked them carefully away. He looked at Brock and said, "I am going to make a recommendation, Mr. Brock, that neither your employers nor my neighbors are going to like. I suggest that this *is* publicly owned grass. I think the best course for everyone will be to leave this man and his sheep strictly alone. He will be gone in a few months and from a practical viewpoint I would think it highly likely that his employer, or employers, will hire cheaper labor next year. I think we all would be well advised to wait until next year." He stood and said, "George, we have that paper to serve while we are down this way. Mr. Brock?"

"I'll stay. Thanks, though."

George did not look too happy with his kinsman's opinion but he didn't argue, and I began to think that this mild and ordinary little sheriff might be more *hombre* than I had given him credit for.

"Thank you for the coffee, Mr. Priest. Good day, sir." He offered his hand and I had no hesitation in taking it.

When they left, Brock helped himself to a refill and shrugged. "Too bad it couldn't have been that easy."

"I can't blame you for trying." I grinned. "The sheriff gives good advice, doesn't he?"

Brock made a face. "That kinda depends on your point of view. I don't know that my employers will share it."

"Well, I hope they do. I'd enjoy a real lazy summer with no one coming around to bother me."

"I'll tell them your preference when I report," he said drily.

"Do that," I agreed. "It could save them a bunch of manpower and money."

He looked vaguely troubled and I almost felt sympathetic toward him until I remembered that if the Association did take Sheriff Herring's advice it would leave the field too open next season when there might be some easygoing Basque or Mexican kid in here trying to make a living and get himself a flock started. If the good old boys in the cattle trade up here were going to come up against a sheepherding man it might just as well be with a woolly bear like me as with someone not used to the rougher games. And I hadn't the slightest doubt that I would still be here at the summer's end.

"How about a bite of lunch," I invited.

Brock gave me half a smile and went to get his contribution from his saddlebags.

CHAPTER 11

I spent another couple days without hearing more from either Brock or the sheriff and my supplies were getting low. It was about time to head for the nearest town and I didn't even know where it was. That gave me enough of an excuse to go visit the lady with the eggs for sale, and I decided to take it.

I had wandered up onto the hill enough by then to know I could take the sheep up there and leave them out of sight long enough that they shouldn't be disturbed even if someone came prowling while I was away so I drove them up afoot—it was tough climbing for a horse in spots, especially the route I'd chosen to take—and left Beggar in charge.

The sorrel was the faster of my two horses so I chose him to make the run around the hill. I could have taken the flock with me, of course, and headed for town right from the woman's ranch, but I didn't want to give Brock any legal excuses for troublemaking in case she objected to me trespassing on deeded land.

The sorrel hadn't had any hard work of late so he was well rested. I put a good sweat on him and was there by midmorning.

The woman was not in sight when I rode up although there was a hoe dropped in the garden and some pools of water between the rows that hadn't had time to seep into the soil yet. She showed up in the doorway a moment later, and she had that rifle in her hands again.

I fingered my hat brim toward her and said, "I thought we'd been through this once before."

"I thought it was someone else." She uncocked the weapon and set it out of sight. "Get down and come inside if you like. I suppose you want more eggs?" When I nodded she said, "I guess being poor means I can't be proud too. I can't afford to turn the money away."

Hell, we weren't talking but about a dollar. A person would have to be in powerful need to give up his pride—or hers—for a single coin. The question was whether the thing needed was the money or an excuse. I tied the sorrel where she had told me the first visit and went into the house. She was already preparing a potful of coffee to put on the stove.

"You can hang your gunbelt over there too," she suggested when I put my hat on a peg.

"I'd rather leave it on, ma'am. I don't want to offend you, but I'd feel funny without it in place."

She gave me a half-disgusted, half-puzzled kind of look and said, "It's true then what Arlo said about you. You really are a hired gunfighter."

"No, ma'am. I can go if you'd be more comfortable, though."

She stood there by the stove looking at me for a little while. She seemed to be waiting for something. Finally she said, "That's it? No long-drawn explanations or defense? That's all you have to say about it?"

I shrugged.

"He said you are a sheepherder too." She flipped that word off her tongue like it tasted of bile.

"I do herd sheep," I told her.

She tossed her head with what seemed to be exasperation and muttered a word that I would not have guessed her to know, much less to have used. "Sit down then. You're the only male I've seen this year who seems capable of carrying on a reasonable conversation with a woman."

"All right." I took the same chair I had used before and she began dragging out silverware and small plates to put beside the empty coffee cups. From her food locker she produced a coffee cake with sugar icing and raisins on top.

"It looks like you were expecting company," I said, "but a minute ago I'd got the idea you were expecting a different sort of company, the kind you point a gun at."

"Sometimes when I'm upset or just can't sleep at night I get up and bake." She gave a short laugh that held little humor. "The past few days I've been gorging on pies just to get rid of them. By the end of the week I probably won't have a stick of dried fruit left in the pantry."

"It's a pity I didn't know that before," I said for the sake of politeness. I don't care much for sweets but most women seem to like having their efforts appreciated. I did not exactly expect the response I got.

"Pies? You want pies? Ha!" She opened the food locker again and plunked three of the things onto the table in front of me. "Is that enough?"

"Yes, ma'am, quite enough." For all I knew she might could produce as many more of the things from in there.

I must have looked a bit startled for she said, "Oh hell, I'm sorry." She took a chair across from me. "It's a shame I can't afford to hire you. I know a person or two I'd like to have shot."

"It wouldn't do you any good if you did hire me," I told her. "I'm really not a smoke artist."

"That isn't the way Arlo tells it."

"That probably isn't the way Arlo *heard* it either but it happens to be the truth. Your friends in the Association might like to have it believed, though, in case we come to a shooting disagreement."

Her lips curled until I was sure she was tasting bile now. "There are no friends of mine in that crowd. Do you know what that Greenough has done now?"

There wasn't really any need for me to shake my head. I doubt I could have stopped her from talking about it short of walking out on her.

"It isn't enough that he already has me in a wringer as it is with no husband and no hands and no way to get my cattle to market and no money unless I can. No, that isn't enough. *Now* he goes and buys a note for the little I owe at the store. He actually went and filed papers on me. That's what Arlo was here about. Sat in that same chair you're sitting in, like butter wouldn't melt in his mouth, the sneak, and that cousin of his right beside him, and tried to tell me how sorry he was but he didn't have any choice once the paper was filed. Him and that Daniel Hancock at the store. I wouldn't have thought they would do things this way, but they're both right in there with Greenough. They probably expect to get a part of my herd after the auction."

She was feeling genuinely hot about it. As much frustrated as angry I would have bet and little or nothing she seemed able to do about it. It was a genuine shame all right, but I couldn't see that jumping in with a lot of talk and sympathy was going to help any. "Coffee's boiling," I told her.

"Oh!" She gave me an angry look that clearly said she expected something more than that. She went to the stove and took her time fussing over the pot with her back turned toward me. When she brought the coffee to the table she was more composed. "Tell me about sheepherding," she said in a rather complete change of subject.

"The work isn't hard and it lets me stay away from people," I said.

"Ouch. You might claim you're not a gunfighter but you sure can shoot from the hip, mister. All you wanted here was eggs, right? And you got a bellyful of my fussing."

"My oh my but you're a sensitive one today. If I decide to insult you I can do better than that. And if you'd pour the coffee I might find a reason to compliment you. Okay?"

She sighed and poured and sat. "All right. I'm sorry."

"You said that once already." I cut myself a wedge of dried peach pie and it wasn't bad. I praised it for what it was and maybe a little beyond.

"Thank you." After a minute she asked, "Are you *sure* you aren't a gunman?"

"I'd know about it. Honest."

"But you might not want to admit it," she suggested hopefully.

"One of the nicest things about living the way I do and not being beholden to any man—or woman—is that I don't have to lie to anybody, ever, on any subject. I like it that way."

She dropped her fork onto her plate though she'd scarcely touched the piece of coffee cake she'd taken. She sat back and lowered her chin and gave me a long look. I hadn't forgotten how green her eyes were but I was struck by it all over again just the same. "You know, I almost believe you."

"Most don't," I said. "I guess if they can't imagine themselves doing that way, they can't see anyone else doing it either." I grinned. "It can be awful useful. Tell somebody the exact, sure enough truth when he's expecting you to lie and he'll disbelieve you every time. Works out better'n a lie ever could."

She laughed. "I believe it really would. I will have to remember that, Mr. Priest." She looked as if she had just reminded herself of something. "Arlo told me that Jude is short for Judas. Judas Priest. Is that really your name, Mr. Priest?"

"Kinda hard to accept, isn't it?" I said with a laugh of my own.

"I'm used to it myself, of course, but it seems to take most folks a while. After a time you don't hardly think about it anymore."

Now that was one little aspect of truth-telling that I hadn't mentioned to her, and that was to not really answer the same question that has been asked. But like everyone else she figured I had just told her that it was my real, born-with name, although that was not at all what I had said. But I hadn't lied to her. I just neglected to correct her when she came to a false conclusion.

"More coffee, Mr. Priest?"

"Yes, ma'am, I'd like some. And some eggs and some directions to town. I need to go in for supplies and don't know where it is."

She provided all three—the town was about half a day's ride north and west—and we talked for a time about inconsequential things and when I left I believe she was feeling a little less upset than she had been.

It was going to be quite a blow to her, though, when Arlo Herring brought a crew of men out to gather her stock and drive them off for auction. That would almost certainly signal the end for her here because a beef outfit can't hardly get along with neither beef nor men to handle them. It did seem an awful shame, too, to let such a well-built place and well-managed herd fall into ruin. John whatever-his-name-was had built well here, and now the product of his work was dying.

I stopped the sorrel horse short, no doubt making him wonder what was up that he would be dragged down from a hand gallop and then jigged forward again so soon, but I snapped my fingers and cussed myself some. I'd sat there through all that conversation and laughed to myself about how clever I was being in telling her about my name, and I had never once remembered to ask hers. I felt kind of stupid as I rode back toward my woollies.

CHAPTER 12

With the sheep to slow me down it was late the next day before I had the town in sight and at that I was pushing them. I laid over with them for the night and then drove them in close to the town buildings before I tried to do any business. It has been my experience that even such a cow-country honorable thing as sheep clubbing is something the cattlemen prefer to do in private. I did not think the wethers were in any danger in plain view of a couple hundred townspeople.

The place was called Wolf Creek, which led me to believe there must have been some of the creatures in the area at one time even if I was having no trouble with them now. There were enough houses and businesses to indicate a population of three or maybe four hundred, and a telegraph wire snaked a shiny, spindley-poled path in from the hills to the east. The town was situated on the far side of a creek that I assumed was called Wolf.

I left the sheep on a small flat of drying grass and crossed the wooden bridge to the business district. Most of the houses were spotted here and there on the slope of a hill beyond.

It could be no secret that I was here with a flock of sheep, but I decided I might as well try to buy my supplies locally before I wired Blackburn to ship some in for me. And maybe it was not completely by chance that I went into a sprawled-out mercantile with a sign in front reading "D. Hancock, General Mchse." As I recalled it was a Daniel Hancock that the woman had mentioned owing.

The inside of the store was a profusion of kegs and crates and bales with one large area reserved for open counters and stacked shelves. A middle-aged man with a small mustache and a pot belly came over to see what I wanted. His offer of service was delivered in a nasal, New England-sounding voice.

"I'd like to outfit here if you want the business," I told him.

"Cash?"

"Uh huh."

He smiled. "Have you ever seen a merchant refuse cash customers, sir?"

"A good many times."

"Then I suggest they were clerks, not merchants." He pronounced it "clarks" and at first I didn't realize what he'd meant. "Ah yes. You must be the shepherd who threatens to destroy our economy. Odd how two species can graze side by side elsewhere but not here, isn't it? No matter, though. I do not propose to take sides in something I know nothing about. If you have cash you are welcome to buy."

"Good. I'll need a receipt." He nodded. Blackburn could reimburse me later, and since I make a fair amount of money and have few needs to spend it on, it would cause no inconvenience. "If you have a paper and pencil I'll write out the order."

He produced them, and I took a stool at his counter to put down what I thought I would need and a few things extra. The extras I set down separately.

"Most of this can go into the pack bags on those horses out front," I told him. "These things you can bag up for saddle carrying if you don't mind."

"Of course."

"You are Daniel Hancock?" I couldn't help asking.

"Yes."

"Funny. I thought you'd have kinda a different attitude."

"How so?"

"After hearing what you did to that widow woman south of here I kinda thought you were taking sides in a number of things." Maybe that was a dumb thing to throw at the man, but I have never been strong on tact.

Hancock clouded up and looked ready to spit. "I will thank you, sir, to *not* link me with that disgusting business."

"Maybe somebody gave me the wrong idea," I offered.

"Someone most assuredly did," the merchant declared. "Jay Pyle offered to buy that debt. He said the LG wanted to help the lady, to make sure her credit was clear while she was having difficulty. It was a simple business deal." He seemed to have a little difficulty spitting out the rest of it and I got the impression he was almost ashamed of saying it. "I would have refused the offer had I known the real intent, sir."

"I'll take your word for that, Mr. Hancock," I said, although I might have had a few reservations there. "But you've thrown some new names at me. I can guess that the LG would be Greenough's outfit, but who is Jay Pyle?"

"Pyle is foreman of the LG. As far as the town is concerned he *is* the LG. The actual owner does not come out into the hinterlands."

That would account for at least part of Hancock's—and quite possibly others' as well—lack of unquestioning support for the area's biggest owner. Absentee ownership is just not calculated to stimulate local pride.

"Well now, I sure appreciate you setting me straight, Mr. Hancock. It's bad enough to think poorly of a man, but it's even worse when the opinion isn't deserved. I'm glad to find I'd heard things wrong."

Hancock smiled and bobbed his head and seemed quite pleased. He smoothed and resmoothed the paper I had written my order on and bobbed his head again, and I believe he was embarrassed as well as pleased. "I will have your order loaded within the hour," he said.

"I'll be back then," I told him and left.

The sunlight was bright after being inside the store, and I stood on Hancock's narrow section of covered walkway to look around for a moment. The first sign I saw that was of interest to me was the telegraph office. There were a few other things I wanted to do while I was in town, but I decided I might as well let Blackburn know his sheep were all right and that he needn't worry about not receiving a supply order.

Since a telegraph message is only as private as the mouth of the man who sends it I didn't go into any glowing details in my message—not that I likely would have done so anyway—but just told Blackburn there had been no losses from the flock and that I would be buying my supplies in Wolf Creek until further notice. I sent the telegram collect. It was, after all, Blackburn's business.

Sheriff Arlo Herring had an office in the small building that served as a courthouse for whatever county this was. The sheriff was in, his feet propped up and a magazine in his hands. His cousin/deputy, George, seemed to be out. The duly elected lawkeeper gave me a pleasant enough nod when I entered.

"Good morning, Priest. Looking to have me comb some burrs out of your wool today?"

I shook my head. "Sorry, sheriff. No fees today. I generally handle my own comb."

He set the magazine aside and placed his spectacles on top of it. He let his feet drop heavily to the floor and sat upright with a squeaky protest from the spring in his swivel chair. "That's a pity. I was thinking of advertising a special this week on warrants and assorted writs. Very slow trade around here."

"It promises to get better," I told him. "The boys in Cheyenne won't lie still too long. They like to think people should jump when they bark."

Herring sighed. "You may be right but I've been getting quite used to peace and quiet. Most of the time this is a fine job for a lazy man."

"As far as I'm concerned you can stay that way."

He squinted at me. "You aren't having any trouble, then?"

"Not the least bit," I assured him. "My sheep are getting fat, which is just the way I like it."

"That's funny. . . ." His voice tailed away and when I asked what he meant he just shook his head. "Nothing. Just a wayward thought. What is it you want then if there isn't any sheep war going on?"

"Something else, sheriff. After you left my camp the other day you served another paper on my, uh, neighbor down there. I wanted to ask you about that."

Herring grimaced. "That sort of thing is a helluva way to earn a fee, I'll tell you. I don't like that sort of business, but it is the law. I had no choice about it."

"It does seem like a pretty sorry way to finagle somebody out of a herd of beeves," I agreed with him.

"There isn't *that* much at stake," he said, "though I suppose in the long run it will come to the same thing as if there was. For right now, though," he shrugged, "the woman stands to lose maybe eight steers if I can find that many. A dozen cows otherwise. I'll have to bring in enough to cover the note plus costs, of course. My fees and court costs and whatever I have to pay for someone to gather them."

"Eight steers? She can't owe much then."

He shook his head. "A hundred fifty-six dollars is all."

"Then Greenough doesn't have her down and out yet."

"Not on the surface maybe, but he does. Hancock would've carried the debt quite a way, I'm sure. He gave me hell when he found out I was serving a paper based on it." My opinion of Hancock raised a notch. The merchant hadn't been blowing his horn as much as I'd thought. "But now that it's come to this I doubt he would give her any more credit," the sheriff continued. "For that matter, it wouldn't do anyone any good if he did. He'd only end up losing whatever he advanced her."

"She'll still have a pretty decent herd out there, sheriff. There should be several hundred stock cows and their this-year increase. They have to be worth a good bit."

Again the sheriff shrugged. "On paper maybe. Don't forget, the official roundup has been completed. Estrayed and unbranded animals become the property of the Association. That's the law here. Selling them pays the cost of their enforcement and range management divisions. I doubt you could find many calves still with cows wearing her brand, and John cleaned out most of the steers last year.

"Even if there was something other than her stockers for her to sell she couldn't hire anyone to gather and market them. She doesn't have cash to pay them nor credit to provision them, and she wouldn't be able to find hands if she did. Anyone who works there might find himself on the blacklist, and I don't know of too many fellows willing to give up their whole livelihood just to help one grass widow who may or may not have a husband turning up at the door someday. So figure it yourself. The woman is through whether she wants to admit it or not."

"Sleep good at night do you, sheriff?"

He gave me a thin smile. "Son, I sleep just fine. Like them or not, I enforce the laws. Every one of them. And as far as I know there's not a single illegal thing been done to that woman. If I ever find out different I will take great pleasure in jumping onto somebody with both bootheels. Until then I will keep my opinions to myself."

"I surely am glad I'm not an officer of the law, sheriff." He raised an eyebrow and I said, "I kinda like being able to call a man a sonuvabitch whenever he earns it."

"The law has its place," Herring said mildly.

"And its limitations. I'm not real fond of limitations." I took my hat off and stared inside the bowl of the crown for a moment. "Tell me," I said. "What would happen if the woman's note was satisfied without it having to go to auction?"

I put my hat back where it belonged in time to catch Herring with a deeply thoughtful expression on his usually bland features.

"Probably very little except to postpone the inevitable," he said finally.

"But it might angrify Mr. Greenough pretty good," I suggested.

"Not if he thinks it through," the sheriff said. "It wouldn't really change anything."

I grinned. "I wouldn't mind putting another burr in that man's hair. What's the tab at this point?"

"I'd think that your presence angers him quite enough already. But if you insist on thumbing your nose at him it would be legal for you to do so, of course. The note is for a hundred fifty-six and my fee for service of the writ is two dollars. Cost of filing is another two dollars. Make it one-sixty even."

"Good enough, sheriff." I pulled my shirttail out so I could get into my money belt. I hadn't looked in there lately but I figured there should be seven or eight hundred in unblown wages yet. I counted out the bills to make a hundred sixty and dropped them on the sheriff's desk.

"Would you like a writ of satisfaction to take back to the lady?" he asked.

From the speculative tightening I could see at the corners of his eyes I could just guess he was thinking about what kind of thank-you I might expect from the lady, but I figured he would likely keep that to himself. As long as he didn't do his wondering out loud I figured he was entitled to think what he pleased. "I would," I told him.

"Wait here then. I'll have the clerk prepare it." He picked up the money and his spectacles and disappeared down the courthouse hallway. I took the magazine he'd been reading and settled myself to wait.

CHAPTER 13

It was a relief to leave Wolf Creek behind me, especially with the pack horses heavily loaded so I wouldn't have to go back in any time soon. It wasn't as crowded or as noisy as many but it was still a town and full of strangers and foul odors and the need to think about others before a person could do what he wanted.

There were a handful of cowboys hooting and calling insults from a distance when I pulled the wethers into a bunch and started them south, but none of the riders offered to come close or start any trouble. I ignored them and pretty soon they went back to their indoor amusements and Beggar and I drove the flock on.

That night Beggar showed some nervousness during the small hours. I carried the scattergun on a little scout around where I had the flock bedded, but I didn't see anything and went back to sleep without deciding if it was four-legged animals or the upright walking kind that had disturbed him. Whichever, there had been no harm done.

We got back to my own temporarily claimed grass that next evening but I held the flock to the left of the big hill and drove them onto the woman's land. I took a chance doing it that way but I wanted to deliver that paper and would not want to leave the sheep unattended again for a while.

There was already a light showing in the house windows when I stopped the flock below the ranch pens and told Beggar to keep them tight. In the evening light with the hill towering behind and the neat yard and garden below, the place was a pretty sight and I enjoyed the ride up to it.

"Hello the house," I called when I was close enough.

The woman came to the door and pulled it open a crack. Yellow light spilling out from behind caught in her hair and softened the outlines of her face. It almost made her look pretty and seemed as well to accent whatever it was about her that kept a man so much aware that this was a woman. I could not see her eyes with the light behind her and so decided for the first time that it was not her eyes that drew the attention so.

"Is that you, Mr. Priest?"

"Yes, ma'am."

"Get down and come in then. I already had my supper but I can fix something quick enough."

"Thanks but I'd better not. I have my sheep on your grass. I just wanted to drop something off here. I'll take the woollies off your place right away."

She pulled the door wider and stepped onto the stoop. "It is too dark to be driving stock anymore tonight. You'd lose some for sure. And one night of sheep shouldn't ruin my grass. Leave them where they are. Or better yet, turn them into the pens. Nothing will bother them there."

"If you're sure, ma'am."

"I am."

"All right. I'll be back shortly." I wheeled the sorrel away and loped him down to the flock. Behind me I could still make out a dim form as the woman crossed her yard to open the gate for me.

I drove the wethers into her pens and they set up a low bleating until they had sorted out the limits of their confinement and had located the long water trough her man had built under the flow pipe from the spring. I stacked my packs and other gear against the barn wall and turned the horses into a small corral next to the barn. The woman watched in silence.

It was full dark by the time it was done. I found her notice of satisfaction in my saddlebag pocket and carried that and the sack of extra eatables with me to the house. She walked at my shoulder without talking, and I liked it that she had not found it necessary to chatter while I was busy.

I held the door for her to go inside and not until I heard the scrape of his toenails on the smoothed floor did I remember that I had brought Beggar into the house without invitation. He is with me so much that I sometimes take him as a matter of course and forget that some people object to the hair and the smell of a dog indoors. I stopped and uttered a short "whoops." "I'll throw him out if you like."

She looked at him and shook her head. "That's all right. He isn't dangerous, is he?"

"He won't bother you."

"He looks mean."

I laughed. He had already chosen a spot on one of the rugs where he flopped and lolled his tongue while he looked the place over. He was putting on his most innocent and inoffensive manners here, and if she thought he looked mean now I wondered what she would think of him when his hackles were up.

"He's mean as a snake, ma'am, but he only does it on purpose. He won't bother you unless you try to hurt me or his sheep. He does get testy then."

She chuckled. "It's a good thing I didn't throw down on you with my rifle this time." She knelt beside him and found the favored spot behind his ears, which he does not allow just everyone to touch. "Eggs again?" she asked while she scratched.

"That'd be nice." I dumped my sack onto the table. "Hancock sent some stuff out to you. He might've felt bad about what happened. He thought the LG was trying to help you when they bought that debt."

"Really? That doesn't sound like him." She crossed to the kitchen part of the long room and fingered her way through the things I'd brought. "Still, don't stare at gift horses and all that. I'm not too proud to use every bit of it."

"There's also this. The sheriff asked me to save him a trip down with it."

She took the paper and read over it carefully. She was certain to be wondering about it but it did not show in her face. "He didn't send any letter of explanation with it?"

"No, ma'am. Just what you have there."

"This really is my day for gift horses then. Hancock again?"

I shrugged as if to say that I didn't know.

She was not overcome with joy or excitement but then she was too bright a woman to think that the slip of paper was anything more than a brief reprieve. After a moment she folded the paper and laid it away in a drawer in the sideboard. "I'll get your supper now."

"All right." I pulled a not too elderly copy of *Harper's Weekly* off a shelf and settled myself in the armchair nearest her reading lamp. Beggar got up with a short grunt and padded over to drape himself heavily across my feet. From time to time while I read I noticed the woman looking over toward where I sat with the dog. I suppose we presented a rather domesticated appearance there, one that might have drawn either laughs or disbelief from certain cattlemen entitled to a somewhat different vision of us. I suppose it would have taken only Arlo Herring's spectacles and a pair of house slippers to make the picture complete. I visualized it myself and almost laughed out loud.

I wasn't laughing a few minutes later when the woman carried a cup of fresh coffee to me. She set it carefully onto the smoking stand beside the chair, used two fingers to gently tug the magazine out of my hands and let it drop to the floor with a loud flutter of disarranged pages. She put her hands on her hips and gave me a searching look with those disturbing green eyes. "Why do you have to be a sheepherder?" She muttered a rough oath and let herself flow down onto the chair nearby. Beggar grunted in protest and shifted aside to make room for her feet.

She might've been awfully thin but at this distance it was neither distressing nor detractive. Something caught in my throat and I began to wonder if annoying a certain cattleman was the only reason I'd gone and paid that bill. I was thinking it a pity that she had a husband somewhere. Or might have one.

I looked at her for what seemed a long time. Every contour and color of her face seemed exceptionally sharp and clear to my eye.

"In case you are wondering," she said, "I feel sure in my own mind that I'm a widow."

"I was wondering," I told her truthfully. "And if you're wrong?"

"I would go back to him. By choice, not duty. He was a fine man."

"And a fortunate one."

She smiled. "I'll take that as a compliment."

"It was intended as one."

"Good." She curled herself into the chair and closed her eyes, and I desperately wished I could be free to kiss her. I believed, perhaps wrongly, she would have welcomed it if things were different for her.

My wanting of her became almost too much to bear and after a while I looked away. "Look, I . . . think we should eat now . . . or wait until breakfast."

Amusement, but a warm and not derisive amusement, pulled deeper crinkles into the flesh at the corners of her eyes and she said, "Then I think we should eat."

I nodded and tried with absolutely no success to concentrate on *Harper's*.

CHAPTER 14

I left the next morning to drive my sheep, Howard Blackburn's sheep, around to the west side of the hill. At parting she had been pleasant enough. She was warm without being effusive. It was clear I could return but she did not demand it. She was much woman and one unlike any I had known before. My thoughts were full of her as I trailed behind the slow-moving flock, and the memory of her was strong.

"I hope you're in a mood to work today," I told Beggar. "'Cause I'm not." He trotted beside me with the remaining portion of his tail raised like a flag and his senses alert to the world around him. I was not so alert myself, my thoughts being turned inward and my body conscious of a tight sensation of hollowness in the wanting of her.

The things I had cached near my camp were undisturbed, which pleased me. I know better than to leave anything in an unguarded camp that is not easily replaceable—and I have become adept over the years at hiding my caches—but more than once I have had the annoyance of having to replace cooking gear and such.

For some reason a cow waddy destroying a sheep camp generally ruins things on the spot instead of carrying them off, and sometimes I just marvel at the trouble one of those boys will go to. It takes considerable effort and a lot of determination to crush a steel pot and partly because of that I always make it a point to buy nothing but the best and the toughest.

This time, though, nothing had been bothered, and I set my camp up to my liking again.

The sheep spread comfortably across several acres of the good grass and Beggar alternated between watching them and nosing into my camp activities. I had finished setting up and was about to fix some lunch when the big dog gave a brief warning growl and disappeared into the hillside brush. Since he was not moving to put himself between the sheep and whatever it was he had detected, it had to be a human intrusion. I pulled the shotgun from its pack-saddle scabbard and slipped uphill to a nest of bare rock that had been one of the reasons I originally set up here.

For a long time I saw and heard nothing except the sheep and some birds and a whistling noise that might have been a marmot. A steady wind made it hard to hear anything out of place but after ten minutes or so I was fairly sure I had some guests arriving by foot farther up on the hillside. I snugged down among the rocks and lay without moving and after a while I spotted them.

There were two, both carrying long guns as well as holstered revolvers. They were slinking along in their best imitation of red Indians on the warpath but either they were an awful lot better on horseback than they were in the woods or they were awfully poor at cowboying. They ignored or perhaps simply didn't see the one fairly decent line of covered approach that was open to them and moved down too quickly and too close. I would have bet I knew what they were feeling, though, for there isn't much that can make a grown man feel sillier than creeping around like a kid at play, especially if he is sneaking up on an empty camp. I have done it often enough myself to know.

When they were positioned so both were hidden from my camp but were wide, wide open to me I figured they had come far enough. I sighed and aimed my charge of single-ought buckshot and blew the silence away with a shattering blast from the short barrel. A severed tree limb fell nearly onto the head of the nearer of them.

"Right there will do nicely, boys," I called to them. "I have another load in this thing and a belly gun if I need more."

Now those were a couple of startled old boys. Like the saying goes, they didn't know whether they ought to go blind first or afterward. Both of them turned pasty white and even at the distance were shiny-faced with cold sweat.

"Lay your rifles down, boys, and the pistols on top of them. That's nice. You can stand up and stretch now. Be a lot more comfortable. And you might as well walk on down and have a seat by the fire."

I stood up to follow them down and Beggar came nosing out of the brush just beyond and above the farther one. When I saw him I was glad this hadn't come to a fight. I hadn't known just where he

was and I might have hit him if they'd turned things loose. I think
seeing him there scared them worse than my shotgun had, and really I couldn't blame them. His teeth were on display and he was
ready. I wondered if they might have heard what he did to that
fellow back in Evanston.

"Ease off, boy," I said and he came down a little although without letting his attention leave them the least bit. "You can go ahead
now," I told them.

They stumbled down the hillside to my fire, dividing their attention between Beggar and the open end of my shotgun barrels.

"Now what?" the nearer of them asked once they'd reached the
fire.

"Have a seat, boys. Make yourselves comfortable," I invited. They
looked a little pained about it but accepted my suggestion.

I settled in my usual spot with Beggar crouched alertly beside
me and took a moment to look them over.

Both of them looked more like riding hands than gunhands but
neither was of the young-and-dumb school like I'd seen on the way
up here. These two were old enough to be shaving out of need instead of just pride, and one of them might've had time to wear out a
cheap razor already. The younger of them would've been well into
his twenties and the older probably in his thirties. Both of them
had gloves tucked under their belts, which almost certainly meant
they were just cowboys being pressed into a little catch-as-catch-
can sheep-running service. It was nice to know the opposition
hadn't gotten real serious yet.

The older one looked the more dangerous of the pair. He had
that lean and sun-dried look of a fella who'd come up the long trail
from Texas a time or two in the past and so should've had himself
some educational experiences along the way. That is a trip a man
couldn't hardly make without learning just how much grit he has in
his craw.

The other one was a little beefier and ruddy-faced. He was wearing a pair of woolly chaps with wide, floppy legs unlike the scarred
and scratched grain-leather leggings the older one wore. If I was
going to guess I would've put the younger one as being from an
easier part of the country, maybe from Oregon or even Minnesota.
Not that they don't grow some pretty salty old boys in the grassier
parts of the country—one of the toughest fellows I've ever seen

came from Brooklyn—but this boy just didn't have the same look of down-deep steel that the other one did.

I laid the shotgun across my lap and took my time about loading my pipe and setting it properly afire.

"What's your names?" I asked between puffs when the thing finally acted as though it wanted to draw right.

"Popper Morgan," the older one said. "This's Charlie Fielding."

"Popper," I repeated. "Like in brush popper?"

"Uh huh," he grunted, but not until he'd given me a narrow-eyed look.

This didn't seem the time or the place to be making old-home-week connections so I let it pass, but likely Morgan and I used to know some of the same people and likely we'd ridden some of the same trails. A brush popper is a fellow who busts his way through the thorny brasada in South Texas chasing wild cows, mostly with dogs and short ropes and tired horses, which is where and how I had started myself once upon a time.

"Charlie," I said, "whyn't you go find yours and Popper's horses an' bring them over here where they'll be handier later."

"You'd trust me to go off by myself?"

I grinned at him. "You can find your way without your hand being held, surely."

"Yeah, but . . ."

"Aw, I know what you meant. Hell, boy, if I was gonna shoot y'all I'd've done it already." I shook my head. "Makes too much of a mess around camp. All that blood to bring flies and everything. Look, if you're so scared you're gonna run out on your partner now, you go ahead and run. Otherwise do what I asked you and we'll talk a little while an' then you can go tell your boss what happened here. All right?"

He stood up although he looked a little confused. He looked at Morgan and gave him a halfway embarrassed shrug. "I'll be back in a few minutes," he promised, to Morgan, not to me. The older one nodded. He didn't look to be too worried about it, either way.

When Charlie was out of hearing range Morgan asked, "Was there something you wanted to say with Charlie not around?" His face was tight and cold, but there was a thin hint of uncontrolled fear in his tone of voice. He seemed to be working real hard to put a rein on it, and I wondered if my question about brush popping had brought up something he might be hiding from. They tell me a guilty conscience can make a person awfully suspicious, and maybe Popper Morgan could have elaborated on that theory.

The truth was, though, that I couldn't have cared less about his past. I was quits with the brush country myself and had been for a long time. I gave him a short smile and a shake of my head. "Not a thing," I told him. "I just wanta be able to see you boys when you ride away from here."

"All right," he said agreeably.

"You might tell me what you fellas were supposed to do today," I suggested.

Morgan thought that over and apparently decided there was no point in acting hostile while I held the upper hand. Or upper shotgun. I did notice that the gun seemed to be a center of attraction for him. "We were supposed to get the drop on you. Tear up your camp whether you were here or not. Club sheep if we could get hold of you first."

"All in a day's work, huh?"

He shrugged. "You know how it is."

Beggar left my side and slipped away in the direction Charlie had gone.

"I'll tell you what, Popper. I'll give you a fair warning, and you can pass it around the bunkhouse. I don't much like to fight with honest cowboys, and as long as you stick to working cows I'll leave you alone. If your boss wants gunwork done he can bring in some specialists. Them I don't mind swapping shots with."

I gave him a cold smile that did not have any humor put into it. "But in the future I'll just kinda assume that anybody coming near my camp or my sheep with a gun in his hand *isn't* on cow business, and what I shoot will run blood instead of sap." It was Morgan I had nearly dropped that little limb onto so he ought to get the idea.

"All right," he said. He didn't look especially scared and that was just fine. He likely had had enough experience that he would take me seriously, and that was what I wanted.

Charlie came back leading a pair of horses with an LG brand on the near shoulder, which was not exactly a surprise. Beggar was padding along behind him. The horses didn't seem to mind him being there, but the dog sure hell had Charlie's attention. If he'd had any ideas about pulling out a saddlebag gun they were long forgotten now.

"I won't invite you boys to stay for lunch," I told them. "It's probably better if you leave before we find a reason to get mad at each other."

"That's it?" Charlie asked. "You're turning us loose just like that?"

I couldn't help but laugh at him. "What the hell would you like me to do with you? I didn't pack any thumbscrews with me an' I already told you I don't feel like shooting anybody today. So g'wan home before I have to feed you or something. G'wan now."

Charlie looked both relieved and puzzled. Morgan stood with a snap in his joints and a thoughtful sigh. Good, I figured. It would get talked around among the LG hands. And any who came calling in the future could have no complaint if they got rougher treatment than this pair.

Charlie handed Morgan his reins and the brush popper swung onto his horse and sat waiting for his partner. Charlie hesitated a moment, looking mostly at Beggar instead of me.

Finally he let it out. "What about our guns?" he asked.

"I kinda like them where they are."

Morgan didn't say a word but Charlie managed to look downright aggrieved. "I've got two months' pay in those guns," he said.

"Uh huh. Teaches you something about the value of a dollar, don't it?"

"But . . ."

"Shut up, Charlie," Morgan said wearily. "Think what you're leavin' with instead o' what you're leavin' without."

Charlie still didn't like it but he shut his mouth and followed when Morgan wheeled his horse away.

Me, I watched them out of sight and then put my lunch on to cook. Those extra guns would give me something to do during the afternoon. I'd need to find four good places to stash them here and there on the hillside in case I might have need of some spares sometime in the future. In the meantime I sat by the fire and scratched Beggar's ears and finished that pipeful of fresh tobacco.

CHAPTER 15

I wanted to leave Beggar to watch the wethers, take a little ride around to the other side of the hill and knock on the door of her house with my hat in my hand. Oh how I did want to do that. But there was no way. Instead I kept one eye on the flock and spent my time puttering around camp, hiding everything except just what I needed to get along for a few days.

After supper I smoked and bragged to the dog about how fine that woman was—though I did stop once to snap my fingers and cuss some—her name *still* hadn't come up and I'd been too fuddled to ask—while I waited for darkness.

Once it was full dark I piled the fire high with fresh wood and laid a little self-feeding ramp of the stuff so it should burn for several hours. That done I chirped to Beggar and we gathered the flock ready for a bit of night herding. I took all four horses also, and we crossed the flat to the closed pocket I'd found before.

The sheep hadn't been in there before and they were reluctant to enter now when they couldn't see what was ahead. Beggar put on a flurry of nipping and yipping, though, and convinced them they really wanted to go in.

I turned the horses into the pocket too and carried the shotgun back to the narrow entrance where Beggar and I could keep a watch during the night.

It turned out to be a long night but a quiet one except for some restless, unhappy sheep at our backs. I was able to doze off and on so I didn't mind it too badly.

We took the flock back across the flat before dawn in case anyone might be watching at first light, and I built up my fire to cook breakfast in camp. That first cup of coffee tasted awfully good, too. I don't really mind those long night watches except for that one thing. I always wish I could have a pot of hot coffee close to hand, but there's no way without showing a light.

I napped a little in the afternoon and did the same thing again that night. Just because no one had come a-calling that first night did not mean they would stay away the second also.

Along about midnight I was glad I had gone to the trouble, loss of coffee and all. The moon hadn't much more than disappeared behind the hill that was now at my back when old Beggar gathered his legs under himself. He bumped my thigh with his nose and whined a little to make sure he had my attention.

"I hear you, boy," I whispered. "Take me to 'em, fella."

He ghosted ahead onto the grass and I had to hustle to keep from losing him in the darkness. Even so he had to stop every so often to keep from outrunning me, and each time he looked back like he was getting impatient with me.

Beggar led me out onto the flat and started south on it but after a few minutes he stopped and stood with his muzzle up and nostrils flaring. He didn't seem to know which way to turn, which meant there would be riders coming from both ends of the grass. They probably figured to meet with me and the sheep between them.

Now I didn't know this crowd, who they were or how many. For all I knew there might be half a hundred of them and all with military experience.

On the other hand, the odds against that were pretty high to say the least. More likely this would be a bunch of pretty good cowhands who'd be plenty experienced at running cows in the dark but not at hunting one man with a gun and a willingness to use it. Even when it comes to chasing a stampede in the dark it's the pony that does most of the work. The cowboy is just a passenger on a wild and wicked ride until the horse puts him into a position where he can do some good.

Anyway, these boys would likely be confused and half lost in darkness this deep, and knowing me and my shotgun were supposed to be here too would put them on edge. I called Beggar in to heel and crept forward slow and easy.

After a while I could hear some soft hooffalls moving in from the right. There was no rattle of bit chains here for sure and if anyone had a squeaky saddle he'd left it at home this night. I walked ahead of the sounds until I could hear more of the same coming in from the north. I was guessing that the two groups would be maybe sixty or seventy yards apart then, with Beggar and me between them but a little farther out on the flat.

Well, it is an old trick and one so simple nobody, ever, ought to be foolish enough to fall for it. But, hell . . . it sounded like a fun thing to try and something I'd never done before. I just settled myself belly down in the grass, tucked Beggar in next to me and held my hands in front of my mouth so the direction of the noise would be a little uncertain.

"There he is. Straight ahead," I hollered.

For half a moment nothing happened. I heard a little blowing and snorting as some horses were snatched to a halt. Someone must've been having trouble for one horse whinnied and a man began cussing.

That must have been enough to put the final grate onto someone's nerves for almost immediately someone in the other group of riders couldn't hold it any longer. He touched off a bright streak of flame and the sound of the shot ripped through the night.

I would guess the other bunch must've thought that first lone shot was mine for their whole crowd cut loose then. There seemed to be five or six of them shooting from that side and for a few seconds there they were firing hot and heavy enough that a body could practically read by the light of their muzzle flashes.

On the other side men began yelling and racing their horses every direction but up, and one or two idiots got so excited they fired back at their own people. For a little while there this whole crowd was having themselves a genuinely exciting time.

Eventually—really I guess it wasn't more than seconds, although it seemed a lot longer—somebody got brave enough to ride out into the center of things shouting and screaming and cussing at them to by God quit or he'd shoot them all himself. Though I think he'd have had to wait for daylight to manage it.

He delivered his message in language plain enough for anyone to understand and the two groups began slowly riding in toward their boss, this time not shooting at each other as they came.

"What the hell was that all about?" the voice demanded. "Well?" Still nobody answered. I couldn't hardly blame them either.

"Which stupid sonuvabitch thought he saw Priest?" He sounded as if he thought he had a whole lot of those out here. "And where's the damn sheep? Has anybody seen any sheep?"

Nobody actually answered the man, but there was some stirring and muttering going on among them now.

"Did anybody actually *see* Priest?" No answer.

"How about *you?*" the voice asked, dripping nastiness. "Anybody hurt?"

It was kinda late in the conversation to be asking that question, I thought. But what do I know about being a boss?

"Got a hole in mah wing," another voice drawled quietly.

"Larry?" someone else asked. "You here Larry?" When Larry didn't answer that same voice said, "Larry was right next to me. I thought I heard him holler. He might've been hit."

"Yeah and he might've let his horse run away with him too," the bossman said sarcastically. "Bunch of damned schoolgirls here. I s'pose we'll have to spread out and look for the sorry bastard. And don't *shoot* each other, will you?"

Didn't sound like a very nice fella, I didn't think, but then I guess he was having kind of a bad night. And I guessed too that it was about time I got out of there. If they were going to be beating the grass for a downed rider it was no time for me to be skulking around in the center of things. I touched Beggar on the neck and began crawling backward with him.

I took the sheep back across the flat before daylight again, moving cautiously and just as quiet as a flock of woollies can go. I didn't want to blunder into anyone that might be waiting there—it wasn't a real likely thing but I wanted to take no chances either— yet I wanted those sheep displayed on the open grass come first light. I figured someone would probably be hanging around within looking distance and I wanted to make sure he saw sheep where they hadn't found any the night before.

Come daylight, which was a long time before I could see the sun from my camp at the base of the easternmost hill, I had a chance to look around. I found one hat, which I ignored, and one gun, which I could add to my hillside collection. If there was any blood on the grass I failed to see it. There was no way for me to tell if their Larry had been hit, or how bad if he was.

Some of the searchers seemed to have found my camp, for the things I'd left in view there had been broken open and ruined. Cans crushed and flour scattered over the ground and a chunk of bacon—it'd been turning green anyway or I wouldn't have left it out—stomped into the ground. They'd made a bit of a mess but hadn't done any real damage, and I had left enough stuff out that they probably thought they had gone and hurt me somehow.

I got a few things from one of my caches and put a pot of coffee on to boil while I tidied up the mess.

I hadn't been showing smoke more than twenty minutes when Beggar warned me there was a rider coming in. He was riding out in the open, though, and I saw soon enough that it was Popper Morgan.

"Mornin'," I called to him. "If you have a cup with you I've got somethin' here to fill it."

He nodded and tied his horse and brought a tin cup with him to the fire. He was unshaven and looked red-eyed and tired.

"I'd offer you some breakfast but somebody got in here last night. Nastied up my eatables, too."

Morgan squatted to fill his cup and poured mine full too. "You weren't here, I take it?"

"As it happens, I wasn't. Sheep move around a lot at night, you know." They don't, but Morgan nodded real serious as if he'd known that all along. "I was off getting them back together," I added. "Then all of a sudden-like I heard a bunch of shooting over here. I guess it's a good thing I wasn't to home at the time." I gave him a good, happy grin.

Somehow that failed to cheer the man. He still looked kinda glum. "You're the one that hollered," he accused.

My grin got wider. "I sorta thought you'd deny bein' here."

"Wouldn't be no point to it," he said with a shake of his head.

"True," I told him and took a sip of my coffee. I brew a fine cup if I do say so myself. Over the rim of the cup I added, "I really thought ol' Brock had more sense than what y'all pulled last night."

"Brock? Oh. The Association man. Don't know about him. I heard he went back down to Cheyenne to powwow with the lawyers or some such thing."

"Really?" Morgan could've been covering for the Association or he could've been telling me that this was LG business now. I couldn't know which and really didn't care. However they wanted to play this I would meet it how it came.

"You know," he said, "you could save us an' you both a lot of trouble if you'd move these woollies somewhere else. Just over into Dakota, say. It wouldn't take much."

"Pyle asked you to tell me that?"

Morgan's eyes jumped up toward mine when I spoke the foreman's name. Maybe I wasn't supposed to know it. "No," he said emphatically. "He'd have a fit if he knew I'd come over here. I'm s'posed to be spyin' on you, not talkin' to you. That's my idea. For me and the boys. We got us a pretty good crew here."

"What's that got to do with anything?"

He grimaced, and I was sure my coffee couldn't be the cause. "This isn't a gun crew, Priest. If the LG has to hire on a crew like that some good hands are gonna lose their jobs to make room for the new ones."

"You among them?"

"Maybe. I hain't decided yet." Meaning, I figured, that nobody better say he would back off from anything but he liked peaceable cow work better than scrapping. I wondered if others of this crew might be reluctant to do more fighting for the LG. From what I'd seen so far their loyalty seemed to be more for each other than for the brand and the people who ran it.

I also wondered about him saying the riding hands would be laid off if a gun crew came in. If that was so, Greenough must either be awful tight with a dollar or must have fairly few of them left.

"Sure seems like a lot of fuss 'n' feathers over a few little sheep," I told him.

"Aw, hell," he said. He definitely looked like he had a bad taste in his mouth. I took another swallow of coffee to make sure I hadn't misjudged that good flavor. "If this bunch stays there'll be more comin' behind them. They'll ruin the whole damn range. It won't be fit for cattle anymore."

"You believe that, do you?" Hell, he probably really did.

"Of course." There wasn't the faintest doubt in that tone of voice.

"Tell me, Popper. You know the brasada." He nodded. "You ever been to Webb County?" It was below the Nueces in the brush country.

"I've been there." His tone wasn't inviting discussion of that area nor of what he might've been doing there, though.

"The last I heard there was five times as many sheep in Webb County as there was cows. And they manage to raise a helluva lot of cows in Webb County."

"Yeah, but that's down ho . . . down there. Everybody knows this grass is different. Sheep ruin it."

I shrugged. "I can't convince you different so there's no point in trying. In a few years everybody will've seen different for themselves."

"There won't be sheep here long enough for anyone to see," he said coldly.

"They're already here, Morgan," I said. "They're going to stay."

CHAPTER 16

It seemed to be my day for having company, after daylight as well as before. Morgan hadn't much more than left before the good sheriff, Arlo Herring, came to call. This time he hadn't brought his cousin/deputy, George, with him.

He got off his horse looking weary and moving much older than his years. "Morning, Priest. I have another tipster claiming you have stolen livestock here." This time he openly sounded like he didn't believe it and wished people wouldn't bother him with their game-playing.

I grinned at him. "You already checked the sheep and nobody cares about a dog. So I guess it must be the horses this time."

"You have papers on them," he said in a bored tone. It wasn't close to being a question.

"Sure. Pour yourself a cup while I get them." I dug them out of the correct hidey-hole and reminded myself I'd have to change that one after he left. He was acting like a straight enough fellow but I wasn't quite so foolish as to take a chance on that. The fewer trusts you offer the fewer you'll have blow up in your face.

When I handed him the bills of sale he gave them a brief pass under his eyes without bothering to pull his spectacles out. He nodded and said, "Fine. I did my duty. But I wish those people would realize that I'm the one being annoyed by all this, not you. Why all the secrecy anyway? You didn't have things hidden the last time I was here."

"You missed the excitement by a few hours, sheriff. I had some visitors last night. Didn't amount to much, though."

His eyes narrowed and the boredom left his expression. "Anybody hurt?"

I shrugged. "I wouldn't know. I wasn't here at the time. I heard some shooting. Didn't have to return any of it." I grinned. "But I wouldn't be too awful surprised if an LG rider or two showed up with a bunkhouse accident."

Herring looked angry. "I told Brock to stay away from that stuff here. I won't put up with it." Of course he might just have been trying to impress me, but he sounded like he meant it.

"I understand Brock's in Cheyenne. This was Pyle's idea."

He gave me a shrewd look. "For a man out in the middle of nowhere country you sure keep track of things."

"It's a fact, sheriff. All I want is to be left alone, an' every time I turn around, it seems, I've got somebody else underfoot. I'm beginning to think I could come closer to lonesome in Wolf Creek than I am here."

Herring looked out toward the sheep. "Well, you did bring a pretty potent magnet with you. It wouldn't hurt my feelings any if you took them someplace else, you know."

"Everybody tells me that."

"Yeah, I'll bet." He threw the dregs of his coffee onto the ground and stood. "Thanks for the break, Priest."

"You won't stay to lunch, sheriff?"

"No, I have work to do. Another double-duty trip down here. The widow lady got that satisfaction, didn't she?"

I nodded.

Herring rubbed the back of his neck. He looked weary and unhappy again. "She isn't going to like this visit any better than the last," he said, "but I guess the sooner it's over with the better."

"What's he done this time?"

Sheriff Arlo Herring spoke a few well-chosen pithy words about Lawrence Greenough and then gave me a wry grin. "If you ever repeat anything about me bad-mouthing this county's leading citizen it'll only be the word of a lousy sheepherder, you know."

"Flatterer," I told him. "You didn't answer my question."

He sighed. "Nothing you can buy her out of this time. Jay Pyle claims he made a verbal contract with Reese last year and that the LG paid the man five thousand dollars for range delivery of all 2R stock cows. Just before John drove those steers away and disappeared, Pyle is saying if Reese wanted to take the money and run it's his business but the LG owns the cows now."

"He has a witness he can take into court with him, I suppose."

"Of course. I haven't talked with the man yet. He's supposed to have worked for the LG last year and the reason they didn't file a claim earlier was they couldn't locate their witness. He's supposed to be on his way up from Denver now. They just found him."

"Hell!" I said. "They'll make it stick, too."

He nodded. "No question about it. Amanda Reese might's well pack her things and leave now. It would save her a lot of trouble if she did."

"Amanda, huh? Pretty name."

Herring looked surprised. "You didn't know her name before? I, uh, assumed you knew her better than that."

I shook my head. "I didn't know it, as a matter of fact. And I'd like to ask a favor of you, sheriff. I hope there's no need to tell her how that note came to be satisfied. I never exactly said so, but I think she got the idea Mr. Hancock did that. I don't see any reason she should be told otherwise."

The sheriff pursed his lips. "I don't know that I'd want to tell an outright lie about it, but I'll go this far. Unless a direct question is asked I won't go volunteering anything."

"That's fair enough." I walked him to his horse and stood by while he put his cup back into his saddlebags and climbed onto the animal. He picked up his reins and said, "So long."

I stopped him before he put the horse in motion. "You might have to make a choice soon, sheriff. The LG is getting *real* anxious about these sheep."

"No choice about it, son. I'll do whatever the law says."

"We'll see." I wished him well, but it takes a lot of man for a politician to resist the kind of pressure a big outfit could bring to bear. He swung his horse away and headed for the far side of the hill.

Damn, but that bothered me. I mean, it is one thing for a cowman to fight sheep coming onto his range. That is a simple matter of self-preservation the way they look at it. Sure they are wrong, but they seem to genuinely believe sheep will destroy the public grass, and I can't fault them for fighting me over it. That is something I accept when I take a grass-busting job of sheepherding.

But it is another thing entirely for a man—any man, in any line of business—to steal, especially to steal from a woman. And this latest LG trick was outright theft. I was starting to get mad with Lawrence Greenough.

The thing was, I didn't know what I could do about it.

I did want to do something, though, and that kinda surprised me.

I don't usually care that much about people, especially someone I haven't known long, but I really liked that woman. Amanda, Herring said her name was. Well, I liked her.

It wasn't just a feeling of obligation for the kindness she'd shown me, either. I fretted about that and gave it considerable thought until I'd satisfied myself that that wasn't the reason. But it wasn't. And I've known enough women that I'm not going to get confused between a bit of desire and a real respect for a person I like. This Amanda Reese was a person I liked and respected too. She seemed too good a person for Greenough and his LG outfit to destroy.

But I still didn't know what I could do about it. I wished I did.

I let the horses graze through the afternoon and took a moment or two to admire how fat and sleek they were staying on this grass. They were in as good a condition as if they'd been on grain lately although they hadn't had any to speak of since I took them off the train at Cheyenne. This country was treating them well.

Beggar and I kept a loose hold on the flock, moving with them afoot as they found new grass. I didn't expect any trouble during the day but I wasn't about to be too trusting of my judgment on that. Even though it was a heavy old pig I hauled my rifle along and a pocketful of cartridges.

I've never favored a saddle carbine. The only good thing you can say about them is that they are easy to carry, and a revolver is even easier. Almost as accurate too. If I'm going to go to all the bother of carrying a long gun it is going to be something that will reach out and do some good, so I carry a high sidewall single-shot action fitted with a Petersen barrel and chambered for a .40-110 cartridge. The barrel is long and heavy and the sights are awkwardly bulky, but the gun is more accurate than I can hold it and it will keep that accuracy four times as far as a little .44-40 saddlegun would reach. That is handy for hunting and at other times as well, and more than once I've been glad I had that rifle made up for me.

The trouble I went to in dragging it along that day was wasted, though, and I was glad enough late in the afternoon to be able to stretch out in the shade and nap before dark. I still wasn't expecting more trouble right away but those woollies were going to spend the night in that rocky cul-de-sac again.

CHAPTER 17

I thought about it and thought about it that night and come morning I packed most of my gear onto the horses and started the sheep moving. If some LG snoop wanted to think I was pulling out, fine. But I'd decided I was going to go visiting with Amanda Reese.

Normally I wouldn't have considered doing such a thing. If there is anything guaranteed to make a cattle outfit lose popularity with its neighbors it is being friendly with a sheepherder, but I couldn't see that this woman had much more to lose in Lawrence Greenough's good opinion. And if there was anything I could do to help I wanted to be there.

And yeah, maybe I had something of a selfish purpose too. Two of them really. One was that Greenough and the Association would have a lot more trouble moving me off deeded land than they would from disputed public land. The other was that I just plain wanted to see that woman again. I hadn't been able to quit thinking about her after I left there last.

I hadn't used the south entrance to the flat since I first scouted the place and I decided it was about time I changed my movement pattern a bit. Any time I trusted myself to be able to figure Greenough's moves ahead of time I'd just be asking for trouble. He could have a rifleman waiting any place along the routes I'd been using, so the best thing seemed to be to go by a new path. It would be farther and slower to take the woollies all the way around the south end of the hill but I decided I'd better do it.

I nooned the sheep out in the open with Beggar there to watch them while I carried the rifle up onto the craggy, bare rock down at the south end of the hill. I ate my lunch out of a can up there and saw nothing but my own wethers and, off in the distance, a very few bovines. If anyone was following the flock I couldn't spot him.

What with the slow speed of the flock and the time I'd taken for looking around it was after dark again before I reached the Reese place, which was just fine by me.

This time, though, there was no warm glow of lamplight in the windows, and I began to get worried. I started wondering if she had pulled out after talking with the sheriff. I realized then that just that fear—and it was a fear, I discovered—had been on me ever since Herring had told me what Greenough was doing. I left the sheep where they were and flogged the blue horse up the slope toward the house with Beggar running at the horse's heels.

"Manda!" I came off the horse in a flurry of summer-dry dust that I could smell but not see in the darkness and in hurrying so I tripped on the stoop and nearly fell down. "Are you in there, Manda?"

I was fumbling for the latch when the door opened, and she was in front of me.

We both stood still for several long moments there and I, for one, felt awkward and embarrassed to've been caught acting so foolish as that.

"You're all right," I said stupidly.

"Yes. I'm fine." She sounded cool and poised and very much in control of herself.

"I . . ." The truth is, I didn't really know what to say next. I stood staring into the blackness that hid her.

"You have the sheep with you?" Her voice was a soft and neutral thing. If she felt joy or worry or welcome I could not find it there.

"Yes."

"Put them in the pen then, Jude. I'll light a lamp and put coffee on the stove."

"All right." I turned. "I, uh, I'll put my gear in the barn if that's all right." I went on to catch up the blue horse and go look after my sheep. I still felt foolish as hell.

Long before I was done she had light in the windows, and it was good to see it there. When I stamped my boots clean and went inside she had a steaming cup of fresh coffee set beside the chair I'd used before, and either she had been working on her hair or she kept it awfully neatly pinned at night. Beggar went straight to his spot beside the armchair and flopped with a satisfied grunt, but I stood for a moment looking at her.

Her face was calm and still without being stiff. I could remember that I had first thought her plain. I could no longer see how I had believed her so. The quiet beauty that was in her ran deep and very strong. Standing before her now I felt coltish and uncertain how I should act toward her.

I took in the clear green of her eyes for what seemed a long time, finally forced myself to break that contact and take the chair she so obviously intended for me.

"You've eaten?"

I nodded. "Recent enough." I hadn't stopped to fix myself an evening meal and my lunch had been scanty but I was not hungry. What I wanted and needed here had nothing to do with food. Seeing her and knowing she was all right had already supplied it.

She poured herself a cup of tea from a cozy-covered pot and settled in the other chair. "I didn't expect you back," she said.

"The sheriff said you're still having troubles."

"And you think you can do something about it."

I sighed. "Not really. Moral support maybe. I wouldn't know what else." Well, that was the simple truth.

If she was disappointed she failed to show it. She nodded quite calmly and said, "It will take several months for it to go through the courts. I can enjoy my home for that long anyway."

"You can't think of any way to disprove it?" I asked. Maybe it was a stupid question but it was a hopeful one.

She shook her head. "No." She gave me a thin smile. "You're assuming Greenough's claim is false."

"It has to be."

"Why?"

I sipped at my coffee, then went ahead and said it. "I can see a man pulling up stakes and running, Manda, if he thought it was time to get out. I can't see him leaving you behind."

She nodded. She seemed satisfied with that, even pleased. And I felt absolutely certain that her man had not pulled out on her. If he was enough man to've earned her loving he was a lot of man. And this was a whole bunch of woman. I just couldn't see him leaving with the money and not the woman if for some reason he had to choose between them.

And thinking like that was apt to get me to assuming things that hadn't been said and presuming things that hadn't been offered. I drained off my coffee even though it was still a little too hot for comfort and stood. Beggar got up and stretched and leaned against my leg.

"My bedroll is out in the barn," I told her. "I think I'd best head for it."

A flicker of some unreadable something passed across her eyes and whatever it was she did not voice it. She rose, gracious and poised, and said only, "I'll get you a lantern to light the way, Jude."

"All right," I said and was conscious that I liked it that she chose to use my name. I wished it was the old name that she knew and used. I would have liked to hear it on her lips, but it was already too late for that. I was known too long and too well as Judas Priest to go back now. Though for the first time in many years I almost wanted to.

She brought the lantern and lighted it, and I thanked her and wished her a good night. There was a longing in me for her to call out as I left but she did not, and I walked with Beggar toward the dark and empty barn.

CHAPTER 18

She was calling me to breakfast by daybreak, and she won some approval from Beggar by cooking the beast a meal of his own. Fried eggs no less, laid on top of some scraps of this and that and served in a crockery bowl. The fool dog liked it, too. He licked it up until the bowl was rattling around on the floor so that I worried he'd break it and then he paid her the compliment of sitting beside her chair while we finished our meal. It was pretty obvious she had his approval.

After we'd eaten I just didn't feel in any particular hurry to get to work. I leaned back and loaded my pipe for an after-meal smoke.

"Can I ask you something, Jude?"

"Sure."

There was dark worry lying deep in her eyes. She opened her mouth but at the last moment hesitated. I could see the change reflected in her expression as she seemed to change her mind with a deliberate will. Tiny strain lines across her forehead and at the corners of her mouth smoothed and faded. When she spoke her voice was matter-of-fact. "I have a few late calves the Association people missed in the district roundup. If you would help me I'd like to brand them before I lose them too. But I can't do it alone."

I thought about prodding her to find out what she'd really wanted to ask, but I didn't do it. It was her business, after all. She could say or could ask whatever she chose.

"You're going to go on trying to work them then?" I asked. "Even if you're going to lose them in a few months?"

She shrugged. "If I can find the help. They *are* mine."

"I don't see why I shouldn't help as much as I can then. The only thing is, I can't go off an' leave another man's sheep untended. They aren't mine to gamble, and your friend Greenough could destroy them all if I'm not around."

"Fair enough," she said with a short, businesslike bob of her head. "I've tried to keep those late-springing cows in fairly close. They're mostly young heifers anyway and not too wild yet. I can bring them in near the place and we can work them in sight of your sheep. All right?"

"Uh huh." My pipe began bubbling with its end-of-bowl juices and I laid it aside. "Any time you bring them in I'll help you work them."

She nodded and seemed quite satisfied with the arrangement.

Now maybe the proper and gentlemanly thing for me to do would've been for me to offer to do all the riding and the searching and the driving for her, but I couldn't hardly do that without breaking faith with Howard Blackburn. Besides which, if this woman intended to try to hang on here in spite of Greenough and his legal finagling she was going to have to be willing to do some of the work involved. And when you thought about it, there really wasn't anything involved here that a woman couldn't handle. She wouldn't have to rope or flank any of her bovines, just find them and push them in close to home. If she couldn't do that much she hadn't a prayer of making it alone here regardless of what Lawrence Greenough might or might not do.

"You won't mind then if I keep the sheep on your grass?" I asked.

"No. Lord knows there's little enough eating it as it is." She smiled. "I'll trade you the grazing for your work."

I suppose I could've taken that for a warning—a fair trade, nobody owing, nobody obligated—but she hadn't sounded as if she meant it that way. It came out as a friendly remark instead of a business deal, and that was the way I took it.

I knocked the cooling dottle out of my pipe and stuck the briar into my coat pocket. I shoved my chair back from the table and said, "It's time I got them out of your pen."

Beggar might've been taken with the woman but he hadn't forgotten his duties. As soon as I was on my feet he was there beside me, ready to go to work.

She inclined her head toward the dog and said, "You don't pay much attention to him, do you?"

"He's more of a partner than a playmate, but ol' Beggar and I get along all right." I bent and gave him a scratch behind the ears. "We've been together a while now."

I left and headed down toward the pens and got to chuckling as

I walked. We'd been together a while, it was true, but it was even longer since I'd last worked cattle. I wondered what Beggar was going to think of those cows and calves.

It was full light by then and had been for a while, and the wethers were bleating a protest at not being allowed to the grass. I swung the gate open and they began bumping and shoving their way out even before Beggar ducked under the bottom rail and got in to where he could work them. I turned them down the gentle slope toward the grass and let Beggar take them on while I saddled the sorrel horse and shoved the long rifle into its boot.

There was a fair amount of grass close to the house, probably because it wouldn't have been used by the usual string of a working crew's saddle stock this year, but I decided that the close-in and protected area might be needed later more than the convenience of it would've been handy now. I took them out a mile or so and let them spread out to eat there.

Once he knew we were where we wanted to be for the day, Beggar took a few swings around the flock. He didn't find any predators close for he soon came trotting back with his tail up and his tongue out and a look about him that said he was pretty well satisfied with the world. I swung down off the sorrel then and loosened the belly cinch.

I sat in the shade of the red horse with Beggar beside me and the sheep spread comfortably over two or three acres in front of us, and I set about doing what has become an old habit with me: I started writing a letter. Oh, I hadn't brought paper or pencil with me. I write a lot of letters but I never set them down on paper. I just compose them in my head, to one or another of the family back home, and it's almost like I really was keeping in touch with them through all these years.

I tell them all the interesting things and all the good things that happen to me and some of the less good things as well. This day I found my letter was mostly about Amanda Reese and her troubles and what she was like, how she looked, and how she acted. There were a fair number of questions in that letter along with the things I could say to be so.

Of course I don't just drift off into daydreaming while I'm writing my letters. I keep my eyes open and a watch out around me while I'm doing it else I probably wouldn't be alive to do it anymore. As it is, though, it helps keep me occupied with something to think about so that I don't get bored or impatient. Possibly because of this I've heard more about boredom than I've felt of it and neither watching sheep nor waiting out a bushwhacker has ever much bothered me.

There were a few hawks in the air, which spoke well of the jackrabbit population and probably explained why the local coyotes weren't anxious to challenge Beggar or a bullet for their supper.

Not long after I got settled I saw the woman riding out to the right. She turned south along the length of the hill that sheltered her place and I soon lost sight of her behind the rolling swells and folds of the ground here. You could see less far here than you might think at first or second glance and I made note of that in the letter I was composing.

I let the sheep drift where they wanted and had no real work to do as they weren't tempted to break the flock and scatter on this smooth blanket of grass. It is mostly in broken country or really poor forage that they will try to splinter into smaller groups. On ground like this the flock will keep itself together and I don't doubt that a person could run sheep untended here if he didn't have cattlemen and coyotes to worry about. They would drift plenty but I imagine they would only need close watching at lambing time, and of course there would be a labor expense at shearing.

I guess I shook my head some when I found myself putting *that* into my unwritten letter. I was starting to have ideas like I was a wool grower myself instead of just a range-busting sheepherder who maybe had more cartridges than prospects. I decided it was time I took a break from my letter-writing so I got up and got the can of embalmed beef I'd brought for my lunch. I opened it and found I didn't really want it all and let Beggar finish the rest of it. This seemed to be his day for treats.

CHAPTER 19

Along about midafternoon I saw the woman coming up with a small gathering of beefy, crossbred heifers and their calves. I signaled Beggar to stay with the flock and rode down to stop her while she was still a quarter mile out. I didn't want the sheep and the cows spooking each other.

She looked pretty proud of herself. And pretty, too, I thought, sitting tall and straight on a leggy gelding that obviously had some good breeding behind it. She rode loose and easy and plainly was as comfortable on top of a horse as she would've been seated in a rig behind one.

The heifers looked good too, well-built mostly red animals with a lot less leg and horn and a lot more meat on their frames than most. They were good milk producers, too, for their calves were fat and lively, with sleek hides and damp, soft-looking muzzles. It was a long time since I'd fooled with calves but I still thought them the prettiest animals ever planted on this earth.

Whoever had worked the official roundup had done an awfully thorough job, though. There wasn't a calf in the bunch that could have been over a couple months old. They were too small to take rough handling and I began to wish I'd brought the blue horse. I didn't know how either of my horses were with cattle but I knew the blue was the steadier, and I sure didn't want a horse bolting with a calf on the end of a rope. They were in for enough of a mauling without that.

The woman's eyes were a sparkling, shiny green and there was a good deal of satisfaction in her smile when she greeted me.

"What do you think of them?"

"They're as good as ever I've seen," I told her without having to exaggerate a bit.

Her smile broadened and she nodded her head in total agreement. "There are more down there but I thought if I spent any more time gathering we wouldn't have time to work any of them."

"You did right," I told her. "No sense bothering them an' then having to turn them loose for lack of daylight. Did you bring your irons?"

"Oh, hell!" she said with a snap of her fingers. "I forgot."

"No harm done. I'll get a fire started while you fetch them. And you can bring some rope and tie strings too. No point in starting with only one rope between us 'cause it purely makes me mad to have to quit something in the middle for breakage of a thing with no replacement handy."

She eyed my saddle and asked, "Where's yours?"

I couldn't help but laugh. "Lord, woman, you've got a short memory. I'm a sheepherding man. Haven't carried a catch rope in years. Now do what I asked you or we won't have time to work even this many."

"Okay. They're all yours." She wheeled her gelding and stuck some iron to him and jumped him from a standstill right into a smooth gallop. She looked back over her shoulder with a grin, and I would have to say she was showing off a bit then.

I eyed the little herd of a dozen or so heifers with calves and a few dry stockers that had mixed into her gather. They all seemed content enough to graze where they were so I slipped down and began building a pile of dried cow patties since there was no wood anywhere near. I had a good supply of chips and the fire going with its thin, nearly invisible flame before she got back.

When she did she handed me a pair of irons that someone had fashioned to stamp her 2R with a single stamp of each iron. That was another of her man's nice touches, I guessed. Most won't go to so much trouble at the forge and then have to waste time drawing each brand with a running iron or maybe an assortment of straight and curved pieces. I laid them into the fire.

"How do you want to handle this?" she asked. She tossed down a coil of rope that was twice as long and half as heavy as anything I'd ever used before.

I took a moment to look at the cows and another to look at her before I answered. There weren't many calves to handle, and she was awful slight.

"You keep the unworked cows in a bunch and make sure that fire stays fueled," I told her. "I can manage the rest of it. And what's all this wad of stuff supposed to be?" I asked, hefting the rope.

"It's a lariat, you dunce."

"You Northerners sure got funny notions of what a rope oughta be then." I flipped it out along the ground and the thing must've been sixty feet or longer, easily twice as much rope as I'd ever in my life thrown. "A fella could get tangled up in all this ribbon and hang himself," I said. I started at the honda and measured back a reasonable length and cut the excess off. "That's more like it. Hell, there's enough left over to make another rope if we need a spare."

She rolled her eyes and shook her head but didn't say anything while I coiled the surplus hemp and gave it back to her. I checked the irons and saw they'd soon be to the ash-gray shade that would be the right heat for laying on a good skin burn without blurring.

"You'll want these," she said and tossed me a handful of tie strings.

I took a look and found they at least made those all right up here. I tucked a couple behind my belt and stepped onto the sorrel.

The rope was thin and more limp than I'd used in the past, and that past was years gone. I knew I would probably show up to Amanda Reese as a rank greenhorn even though I'd had a rope in my hand about since the time I'd been big enough to make a fist. I shook it out and recoiled it and built a loop that I twirled a few times just to get the feel again. It had been a while but at least I didn't hit the sorrel in the head or knock my own hat off or anything like that. Finally I used one of the tie strings to fashion a makeshift neck rope that should help keep the sorrel's head straight on the rope and threaded the butt end of the catch rope through it.

When I tied the catch rope to my horn the woman spoke up. "*Now* what are you doing?"

"Tying it off, of course. What else would I be doing?"

"Are you sure you've worked cows before?" she asked in a sticky-sweet, disbelieving tone of voice.

"Sure I'm sure, woman. It ain't my fault if you Northerners don't know nothin' about workin' cattle. Huh!"

"You're starting to drawl more than usual. You sound like some country-talkin' good ol' drover up the trail from Texas. Did you know that?"

I didn't, but I wouldn't dispute it if that's what she claimed to be hearing. Anyway there wasn't much of a response a body might give to that so I grunted another "Huh!" at her and turned the sorrel toward the little herd of cows.

They weren't wild and moved respectfully away without getting too excited about it so I eased the sorrel toward the nearest calf until he started to look nervous and flipped my loop just once to swing it open before I threw it. By a happy freak of good fortune it hit deep on his neck and I remembered to jerk my slack before he could shake it. I was feeling right proud of myself.

Meantime the woman had gone around to the other side of the bunch and was right there to keep them from buggering and running if the little fellow made a commotion.

I reined the sorrel away from the cows and squeezed him forward, and the calf was dragged along at a stiff-legged bounce, hollering and complaining the whole way to the fire but coming along in spite of himself.

When I had the calf where I wanted him I turned the horse to face him and stepped down to the ground.

I guess I was pretty much holding my breath and crossing my fingers and knocking on wood when I did it for if the sorrel was going to blow up and go drag this calf to death now was the time he was most likely to do it. Fortunately the horse ducked its head and spread its front legs and rooted itself with its eyes locked on that calf, just daring the little guy to try to leave. This one was no stranger to cows.

I went hand over hand down the rope and had no trouble using the rope as a handle on a calf this small. An older one big enough to need dragging down head and heels might've been a problem—I still didn't know if the woman could throw a rope though she'd shown she could ride—but this size I could flank and tie down by myself. As soon as I had him tied I waggled the rope to ask for slack, and the sorrel minced forward a few steps to give it to me and I threw my loop off.

A few slices with my pocket knife took care of castrating and ear marking, and I went to get an iron.

They were pretty hot now, reaching toward that dull red glow that will blotch a brand and maybe cause a slow-healing wound that invites parasites, so I pulled the spare iron to the edge of the fire and took my time carrying the first to the calf, which was waiting quietly now though it rolled its eyes at my approach.

I pressed the iron to its shoulder and counted one-two-three-four to myself while the newly so steer squalled and bawled that it didn't like the treatment. I had just about forgotten the smell of a hot iron on hair and hide, but it came back clear enough now. It was a smell that carried a lot of memories, and I half expected I could look up and see a ring of dust-grimed, unshaven faces above me as a succession of fresh calves was dragged to the fire.

Instead when I looked up I saw clear sky and broad grass and high, green-sheathed hills. And the woman on the far side of her little clutch of cattle.

I would have to say that I liked what I was seeing.

The calf hollered again when I untied him. He scrambled like he'd forgotten how his legs were supposed to work but once he got them under him he made a dash for his mama. She'd been waiting at the near edge of the bunch and now she moved out to sniff him over and give him a nudge toward her flank, and pretty soon he was sucking and seemed to've forgotten the whole experience.

I replaced the used iron on the fire and climbed back onto the sorrel to coil my rope and go get another of the sleek, red youngsters.

CHAPTER 20

We finished with the little bunch of calves before dark, and she carried the irons in while I gathered the sheep and drove them back to the pen for the night.

She got there long before I did, of course, and it was mighty nice to see lights through the windows and know she was in there fixing our supper. I felt relaxed and unhurried and found the whole thing right pleasant.

The lantern she'd given me the evening before was still in the barn so after I'd tended the animals, hers and mine, I lighted the thing and rummaged around in Reese's stuff until I found a wire brush. I sat and talked to Beggar a while and scrubbed the branding irons free of the thin buildup of burned hair and whatever that was already collecting on them. Reese had a half dozen of the 2R irons on the wall but only the two I'd just used needed cleaning. The others had been scraped and rubbed with grease before they were hung for storage.

I'd finished with that chore and was looking around for something else useful I could do when I heard the creak and slam of the screen door and she called, "Wash up for supper, Jude."

I hollered back to let her know I'd heard and said, "Come on, dog. Let's go act civilized." He cocked his head and I told him, "Yes, you too."

I washed at the basin by the spring and reminded myself again to ask her for a towel to put out there. I kept forgetting to do that. At the front door I caught myself pulling my hat off and slicking my hair back. You'd think I was some young and eager buck about to go calling on a girl for the first time.

"What's so funny?" she asked when I went in.

"Huh?"

"That smile you're wearing looks like it's going to turn to chuckles any minute."

"Wha . . . oh. Nothing." I grinned at her. "Just feelin' good, I guess."

"Good." She looked pretty cheerful too. "I always like seeing our . . . my . . . increase. Any calves, really. I just like them." The good humor in her eyes faded at the unintended reminder of her husband, but it did not disappear completely.

"Me too." Beggar and I both began drifting over to the stove end of the big room. "Something smells awful good."

"Ham and eggs. No complaints?"

"Nope. Him neither." Beggar thumped his tail on the floor and the timing was so perfect both us humans got to laughing.

"How come you never fix beef around here, woman?"

"I thought you weren't going to complain."

"Me? Never. I was just asking."

She shrugged and began poking in the skillet with a long-handled fork. "I don't happen to have any, that's why."

"Aw, we can fix that. Soon as the branding's done you can pick a cull. I'll butcher it for you. Hang some of the meat. Salt some. If you want to grease-pack some beef sausage I'll help you do the grinding. Okay?"

"Yes. Jude?"

"Um?"

"Thanks."

"Sure." I helped myself to a cup of her good coffee and took it to the armchair to make another try at reading that *Harper's* I still hadn't had time to finish. I didn't make much progress this time either, though. It seemed I was starting to make some promises about things I intended to do for her in the future, and I needed to do some thinking about that. I was just as happy, really, to be interrupted by her summons to the table.

Later, when the dishes were cleared away and both of us were settled in the sitting part of the room, she raised her eyes from some mending in her lap and caught me staring. "Jude?"

"Yes?"

"You've worked cattle before. Not just a little either. I never saw anybody, not even John, get so much done with so little fuss. You're good at it. And you learned it a long way from here. The way you do things, even little things, is different from the way I've ever seen them done around here. You grew up with it, didn't you?"

"Yeah."

"Why'd you leave it?"

"It's a long story."

I tried to keep my attention on the magazine in my lap, but I could feel her eyes on me. When I glanced up I saw her shudder.

"I can believe it now," she said softly, hesitantly.

I raised my eyebrows.

"Arlo. Sheriff Herring. He told me about you. Not much really, but . . . he said you're a hard man. Like a lone wolf. Cold and quiet and deadly. He said you're very good at what you do, especially killing. I hadn't seen that side of you. You've always been polite and pleasant, even warm, with me. Gentle. But when I asked you that question you turned so cold you almost frighten me, Jude. Right then I couldn't see any more compassion in you than I'd expect to find in a rock wall. Now I can understand more what Arlo was telling me before."

"If I frighten you I should leave," I told her. I knew none of what I was feeling right then was carried into my voice or expression.

She didn't answer right away but took a moment to think about it, sitting quietly with her chin lowered and her eyes locked, huge and green and serious, on mine. Once she had decided, there was no uncertainty in her voice. "No. You don't really frighten me. I don't think you would ever be a threat to me. But I see now how you *can* be. With others." She smiled thinly. "I'm glad I'm not opposing you, Jude Priest. That *would* frighten me. But, no, you needn't leave. I shouldn't have asked such a personal question. I'm sorry."

I nodded and bent my head back toward the magazine. I was glad she couldn't read my thoughts from my expression—old habits helped me there—but the truth was that what she'd said had rocked me pretty hard.

It had been a long time since I'd much cared what anyone else thought of me. And I really had thought I was through with caring. I was finding that that wasn't so. I guess I did care. That really hit me.

Normally if somebody talks about how icy I come across to people at times, I just take it as a compliment. It is useful, for a fact. It helps when I want to be left alone. Right now I did not want to be left alone. And I took it as no compliment if Amanda Reese thought I was aloof.

More, I found myself wanting to explain that I wasn't really that way. Yet maybe I really was. Maybe she or Herring or any one of a hundred other people would know more about that than I ever could. I wouldn't have known what to say to convince her otherwise, and maybe there was no point in trying, for maybe I was the one that was wrong about it.

I felt nervous, too, which isn't real normal for me either, too nervous to sit still with a magazine. I wasn't about to go to pacing the floor so to keep my hands occupied I dragged my pipe out and fiddled with it and loaded it and tamped the tobacco too tight so that I had trouble getting it to draw right. I hadn't much more than got it going when I felt my mouth coming open and I began doing some talking that I hadn't really intended.

"I was raised with cows, all right. Cows and cow dogs and brothers and a couple sisters. Big bunch of family set down in the middle of the brush country of Texas, down below the Nueces. Plenty of cows and plenty of work. I'd be there yet, I s'pose, except later on the old man picked up and moved to Arizona. It was just opening up to cows then. I wasn't sure—I was too young to care anyhow—but the old man might've been run out of Texas. He always was quick to fuss an' feud.

"The old man set up fresh in Arizona and got a good start on putting a decent herd together. Nothing like the stuff your man was breeding here but good, solid range stock. Of course that's beside the point. It don't make any difference what he was raising.

"There was a funny thing happened then. Back in Texas the old man had been raised up with Mex'cans and sheep all around an' never gave it a thought. Not to talk about it, for sure he didn't. The funny thing was that once he got to Arizona he decided he couldn't abide havin' sheep near him no more. Any poor fool that tried bringin' those rank-smelling woollies onto the old man's grass, why he was just askin' for trouble from the old man and all the new neighbors. Got it, too." I gave up trying to keep my pipe going and laid it aside.

"There was another funny thing. Somewhere along the line I'd gone and got the idea things were s'posed to be fair. Man to man, like. I raised an objection one time when they wasn't."

There was a little more to it than that, but there wouldn't have been much point in going into it all. Obregon had been a friend and his sister too, and they were both long dead now. I've never been much of a hand at stopping trouble, and back then I hadn't learned near enough how to handle what I couldn't halt.

"The old man an' his friends didn't like my objections," I went on. "They went ahead and proved how tough they were. I raised some hell about it. Or tried to. Didn't do much good at it. The old man and me got into a helluva fight. Later on I couldn't remember which of us disowned who, but that was the end of that." I made another try at lighting my pipe properly.

The woman didn't say anything for a time. After a moment she came off her chair in a slow, fluid move that looked close to floating. She went to the other end of the room and used a pair of kitchen tongs to fetch a coal from the stove.

She laid her fingers against mine to steady the pipe. They felt cool and very sure. When I had the pipe going she carried the coal back. I was sorry to lose that touch. She went back to her chair and again put those brilliant green eyes on me.

"So now you fight the same war from the other side?" she asked.

I was disappointed when she asked that. Maybe I'd misjudged her after all, read more into her than was really there.

"I don't fight anybody's wars but my own," I said. "I've never taken any animal, sheep or cow, either one, where it had no right to be. The only thing I ask is to be left alone. Anybody does that will get no trouble from me."

"And the man who doesn't leave you alone will get all the trouble he wants," she said.

"That's right too."

"You *are* a hard man, Jude. I'd bet there's only one thing in the world you run from."

"One thing?" I didn't know what she meant. "What's that?"

"I . . . No. I could be wrong, and whether I am or not I've got no right to be bringing it up. Maybe sometime . . ."

She sounded confused, and I decided to let it drop. I shrugged. "Whatever you think best." I got up and snapped my fingers for Beggar to join me. It was time we got out of there, although I wasn't looking forward to the night thoughts and the dreams I might be having this night.

CHAPTER 21

I hope she wasn't embarrassed in the morning. For myself I don't much care what people want to think or even very much what they want to do. For her it was a different matter. She lived here and likely did care about opinions.

The thing was, Arlo Herring and Richard Brock came calling at about a quarter past dawn. I had gone inside for breakfast and was wandering around with a first cup of coffee and lather not yet wiped from behind my ears when Beggar set up a yammer and they stopped their horses at the front door. I had time to towel dry but I imagine the guilty feelings I was having about them finding me inside her home so early were enough to make me look guilty too. And it wasn't like I hadn't been wishing it were so.

If she was upset she was able to hide it all right. She was at the stove and she just leaned back enough that she could see who it was and told me, "Let them in, Jude. I'll get more plates down."

It was hers to decide so I nodded and went to the door.

"Mornin', gentlemen," I told them. "You can come in if you like."

Brock nodded abruptly but Herring took his hat off and spoke a polite hello. Manda greeted both of them by name, which meant that Brock had stopped here before, probably looking for local support against the sheep. I noticed, and they probably did too, that she put their coffee mugs along the side of the table and moved mine from the mirror shelf to a place at the head of the table next to her. I hadn't sat there before but apparently I was supposed to now. It seemed she wasn't one to try and make explanations about things that were no one else's business.

The sheriff hung his gunbelt under his hat, but Brock kept his on. That was all right. My belly gun was in place too.

"Which of us are you here to see?" I asked outright before they even had a chance to start on their coffee.

"Both, actually," Herring said. "We came down yesterday looking for you. Saw you'd pulled out and came around to see Mrs. Reese. It was too late to call last night so we camped a mile north and waited for morning." He smiled. "Mr. Brock was hoping you'd left the area for Dakota."

"You should've known better, Richard." To Herring I said, "Your information seems slow, sheriff. I left my old camp a couple days ago. I'm sure the LG's known about it since I packed. Surely they know where I am by now."

"They don't tell me quite everything they know or do," he said.

"Pity," I told him with a grin. "You'd be amazed."

"I doubt it," the sheriff said. "But I would be interested."

"And what is it you're wanting with me, Richard? Since I'm not running, that is."

Brock grunted but kept his eyes on his coffee.

"Mr. Brock brought a court order back from Cheyenne," Herring said lightly. He sounded kinda amused by it.

"Cheyenne? I thought Wolf Creek was the county seat." Manda clanged the oven door. The biscuits seemed to be ready.

When Brock didn't respond Herring did. "It is, of course. But the Supreme Court sits in Cheyenne. The Association got one of their justices to sign an order for Mr. Brock." He pulled his spectacles from their case and hooked them behind his ears. He brought a paper out, shoved his mug aside and smoothed the document flat on the table before him.

"According to this," Herring said, "evidence has been presented showing that the grazing of wool-bearing livestock—that is, sheep—on public lands endangers forage growth on said lands and, uh, thereby endangers the existence of publicly owned wildlife, which come under the jurisdiction of territorial officials. A restraining order—that is, this here document—is therefore issued pending further presentation of evidence by both wool-growing interests and, uh, wildlife conservationists."

"I suppose Blackburn will have to reply. You'll send him a copy of it?"

"Give me his address."

I did, and he used a stub of pencil to mark it down in the margin of Brock's document.

"Sure is a good thing I don't have those woollies on public land, huh, Richard?"

He didn't look real happy but he finally did decide to look my way. "You'd have been better off if you were, Priest. Then maybe you'd have gone over into Dakota. It won't be dropped here, you know. You won't win this one. I've tried to do this legal, right along the line. Not everybody feels that way."

"Legal? Hell, Richard. You an' me an' every one of those boys down in Cheyenne know your paper might as well be hung in the outhouse where it belongs. That'll never make it through the first appeal to a federal court. The best you could've hoped for would be a delay. You didn't even get that."

"I still say you would have been better off if we had." Brock's eyes were cold, and there was far less humor in him than I'd seen before. I wondered what his bosses had been telling him back in Cheyenne. Maybe they weren't any more patient with legal tactics than Greenough seemed to be.

"We'll see," I told him.

Manda set breakfast on the table and we waited for her to be seated before we pitched into it.

"And what about me, Arlo?" she asked. "You had business here before you knew Jude was over here, you said."

"Are you sure you want your business aired now?" Herring asked.

I got real busy filling my plate and Brock was doing the same. There wasn't any polite or inconspicuous way we could slip out now.

"Jude can hear anything you have to say, Arlo. As for Mr. Brock you can use your own judgment. Obviously I don't know what you're going to tell me or you wouldn't have to say it."

Herring looked uneasily toward Brock and, I thought, a little resentfully toward me. It must've been important, I decided.

"Look," I said, "I haven't fed the horses yet. Why don't Brock and I do that while you two have your talk."

"It can wait until after we eat," Manda said firmly. She passed the biscuits around and not one of the three of us would have dared refuse them. Not and go against that determined, set look she had on her face.

We hustled through a mostly quiet meal and I led Brock outside.

"You look right domesticated these days, Priest."

I gave him a look that said I didn't appreciate that line of conversation, but he ignored it.

"Looks like you moved right in, boy. Um-umm. Cozy." He gave me a leer and a wink and said, "A little skinny but not too ugly. Good is she?"

I didn't take time to think about it. It was coarse and ugly and from the way I'd judged him before it seemed out of character for this tidy and well-controlled man, but I never stopped to think about that. We were walking side by side and I swept a backhanded forearm into his face.

He wound up sitting in the dust with blood starting to run from his mouth. I was about to follow it with a boot when I noticed his eyes. He'd made no move to defend himself nor to pull his gun and he was staring up at me with calm, cold hate.

Too late I realized what he was doing. I don't know if he was aware of it himself, but I was willing to bet that Richard Brock was working up a good reason to hate me so he could turn to the uglier side of the Association's business without violating whatever he held to be right and wrong. I was just willing to bet that was it.

I cussed myself some and stretched out a hand to help him back onto his feet. "We don't talk like that about the lady, huh?"

He looked at my hand, accepted it and came up off the ground. He pulled a handkerchief from a pocket and wiped at the flow of blood that was already into his collar.

"That won't do it," I told him. "Let's feed those animals and I'll help you clean up. There's a washbasin up near the house."

"All right." He didn't sound or look real upset now. He hadn't apologized either, I noticed.

We pitched hay to the horses, and I noticed there was practically none left. There was neither the manpower nor the money for her to have more cut or else bought and hauled in, I knew. Before long she'd have to turn out the few head she owned and let them forage for themselves and maybe keep one up for use in catching the others. If I'd had the time I could've cut more for her—her man had a mower and a pair of rakes parked near a pair of heavy wagons and must have been a believer in hay feeding even before the hard winter's die-up—but I couldn't do that and watch sheep too.

Brock poured out a little grain as well. It was small-kerneled stuff to start with and now was dry and dusty, obviously old. There wasn't much of that left either.

We walked up to the spring and I used his handkerchief to wash the blood off his chin and neck as best I could. It had stopped bleeding anyway.

"I don't think I'll really mind when I have to take you, Priest," he said kinda quietly at one point.

"Okay," I told him. He wasn't really very worked up or emotional now. He meant it. "You'll be working with the LG crew then?"

"Probably."

"They've thought about it some themselves."

"They're amateurs."

"So are you, Richard. You'd make a lousy backshooter."

He didn't get hot or try to tell me how tough he was, and I thought again that this really was a competent fellow. A little too bright for this line of work he was in maybe but indeed a competent man.

"I suppose we can go back in now," I said.

He touched his damp shirt collar, still dark-stained with blood, and said, "I'll wait outside. You can tell your woman I said thanks for the meal."

"She's her own woman. But I'll tell her." He took up his reins and swung into his saddle. "I expect I'll be seeing you again, Richard."

He nodded.

Herring set his cup aside when I told him Brock was mounted and waiting. Herring got his hat and gunbelt and said his goodbyes. When they were gone the woman turned into my side and held herself against me. It felt oddly natural to have her there under my arm.

"I've brought you trouble," I said.

"No. I had that already."

"What did the sheriff have to say?" I asked and only afterward realized that it was really none of my affair and should have been of no interest to me either. But I was concerned.

She shrugged. "Nothing much. Their witness will be here late this week. They're asking for a court date sometime next week. Arlo said he thinks they'll get it."

"You have family? Someplace to go?"

"I'll be fine." She smiled. "I haven't lost yet, you know. And they say the best defense is the truth. I'll try that and see what happens before I start making plans to leave."

She seemed to be taking it all pretty calmly. But maybe she didn't know as well as I did how many lies can be upheld in a court of law. Far as I could see, law and justice are two different things entirely.

CHAPTER 22

She had her cow-calf gather put together a little earlier after having a day to practice in. Or maybe she'd been able to spot them the day before so she could go straight to them this time. Anyway she brought them near my flock early enough that we could noon together.

It was different from what I was used to and I kind of liked it. Since we would be needing a fire anyway to heat the branding irons I went ahead and built it, and she made coffee for us. Usually I allow myself considerable laziness and corner-cutting for a noon meal, but she'd practically dragged along a full dinner. She kept pulling stuff out of her saddle pockets until I thought we were fixing to have some sort of outdoor feast. And all of it was good, too, right down to a scrambled and disarranged but still mighty tasty glob of peach pie that she'd packed out in a lard tin.

When I complimented her on the pie she said, "I'll have to make more. That was the last of it."

"You know, I'd've thought you'd be scurrying around baking day and night with the troubles you've had lately. Now that I think on it, though, you haven't been."

"I hadn't noticed either, but you're right. I haven't had any trouble sleeping through the night either, Jude." She smiled. "Something must have been going right for me lately. But don't worry. I'll do some baking tonight. For you."

I will admit that I enjoyed hearing her add that last part. And I was glad she seemed to be feeling so untroubled in spite of everything that Greenough was trying to do. The last time I'd seen her the house had been cram full of baked stuff. I really preferred the larder the way it was now.

I would have been willing to sit and visit some more. It was pleasant to be there with her under the warm sun with the sheep blatting not too far off in one direction and her cattle tearing grass near us in the other direction. She got up and added some cow chips to the fire, though, and laid her irons on to heat. It seemed she was ready to go to work.

"Okay," I said with an imitation groan. "If you won't let a man rest, I s'pose I'll have to get busy and earn all this good care I've been getting."

She gave me an impish smile. "Then get with it, cowboy."

"Please, woman. I'm a sheepherder. Huh? Shee-eep!"

"Have it your way then. Go to work, sheepboy."

I gave her a swat on the rear that landed hard enough to make her jump, then went to gather up the horses. I'd done it in play, without even thinking, and somehow it didn't seem wrong at all.

She had a few more calves in the bunch this time but still not enough to present a problem getting them done in one afternoon. And there still weren't any big ones in the crowd. Someone sure had done a fine job of working over the Reese herd.

We settled into the routine of the work like we'd been partnered at this for a long time. I don't guess it took ten minutes a calf to rope, throw, cut and brand and be on the way for the next one. It was going smoothly but after eight or ten head had been run by the fire I got some unexpected help.

I hadn't noticed the sheep drifting close in their grazing but now they were near. I'd been afraid if that happened either the sheep or the cows would get scared and try to run out of the county to get away from the other group. As it was they ignored each other. They didn't even seem to be looking at anything outside their own bunch. I could not hardly say as much for Beggar.

Now that old dog was a sheepherder's dream for handling woollies. He did it fast and sure and quiet, and he was better than a pair of armed guards when it came to letting me feel safe and comfortable in camp at night. Good friend too. But he sure hadn't much in the way of experience with cows.

Not that that was going to stop him now. Whatever these creatures were, I was working them, and Beggar seemed convinced that if I was working an animal it just naturally meant that I needed his help to get the chore done. And he seemed to figure he could make up for any shortcomings in experience if he showed enough sheer willingness.

I just finished with a pretty little yellow heifer calf and turned her loose when Beggar came charging in to join the fun. She might've looked strange to him with that short hair but she was about the size of a ewe and he treated her like one, nipping at her heels and running her back to the herd where she soon found her mama and quit bawling. Of course that was where she'd been going anyway so maybe Beggar shouldn't have looked as proud of himself as he did. He came trotting back to where I was mounting the blue horse, and he was waving his tail and wearing a happy look that told me how pleased he was with his own performance. I think he might've decided there was no big difference between sheep and cows.

I rode the blue horse into the bunch and chose my next calf. It was a dark red bull calf that kept trying to hide under its mama's belly. I could've heeled it and dragged it out but that is hard on the animal, so I thought I'd try to haze him away from the cow and make room for a head catch.

When he saw what I was doing old Beggar decided to pitch in and help. Herding is herding, right?

Now it is a fact that a sheep, even a ram, is not a very belligerent animal. They run away from things, any darn things, that threaten them or they think is threatening them or they think *might* threaten them. Even when they are scared and cornered they mostly will stand and quiver and bleat and wait for whatever awful fate is coming their way.

Once in a while a ewe will get brave if her lamb is in danger. Even that doesn't happen very often—for one thing sheep aren't the most maternal of mothers—but every now and then one will put her head down and try to butt her way out of trouble.

A range cow now, especially one with so much as a drop of that tough old longhorn blood in it, is another animal entirely, with or without a calf at her side. They are herd animals and generally easy to drive, but they are notional critters too.

A cow will tackle anything that walks, crawls or swims and what few things they can't whip they can generally fight to a draw anyhow. Given the notion they will fight it out with wolf or bear or anything down the list from there. And a sharp-tipped horn gives them the weaponry to work with.

Beggar, he didn't understand this right off. It didn't take him awful long to learn.

He started after that red calf's heels so he could help me put the youngun where I wanted him. And along came mama.

I don't guess Beggar had been expecting that, and it is a good thing he's so quick-footed. A bit slower and he'd have been a scrap of ragged fur decorating that cow's horn.

He wasn't, but it would have been hard to tell from listening to him. He yipped and kiyied like he'd been stuck like a shoat on a skewer and rolled away so far so fast it really did look for a second as if he'd been hit.

Beggar is no quitter, though. He came up snarling and on the fight, and Manda had a look at the dog with his hackles high. When he puts that hair on end he has a ruff like a prize circus lion. He has the size and the mean in him to make that comparison a good one, too.

He came up ready to turn all of it onto that cow, but this was a new kind of thing he was facing and she wasn't backing off any more than he was. He moved toward her but she wasn't any ewe that was going to turn and run.

I've seen that dog wade hip deep in coyotes and tear into wolves like they were so many pups. Twice I've seen him take on big painter cats—or pumas or cougars or mountain lions or whatever else a body might want to call the same kind of cat—and come out bloodied and gashed but a clear enough winner. Once he scared the cat up a sapling I wouldn't have thought would support a half-grown kitten of the breed and held it treed until I came up to shoot it. The other, a smaller cat than the first had been, he killed outright with no need for me to help.

This time old Beggar'd met his match. This cow hadn't come to play.

When Beggar charged, the cow didn't give an inch. She planted her feet and lowered her head and waited. Soon as he was in range she hooked her right horn at him like a striking snake. He managed to evade it somehow and slashed her ear in passing, but he was sure enough passing and not there to stay. A cow can scrap with its hooves too, and she raked him with a forefoot that he couldn't quite avoid. I would have to call it a one-to-one tie at that point.

Since he happened to be back at that end of the beast, Beggar tried a heel nip. She unloaded with her hind foot with a well-aimed kick for the head. If it had landed that split hoof would've brained him, but this, at least, was old business to him. He darted out of the way and rolled aside when she tried to wheel and use the horn again.

If he couldn't bite he could sure bark, so he danced around just out of range and told her what he was thinking.

Whatever he was saying didn't make much impression on her. The cow stood squared off with him, her head low and eyes straight ahead. Her nostrils were flared wide and there was a slimy-looking rope of saliva drooling out of her mouth. She looked like she was ready to start exhaling smoke and fire any moment.

I figured the education was good for the dog, but I wouldn't want him hurt. It seemed a good time to declare it a draw.

I let go the handle on my loop and let the rope fall into a knot at the honda. I swung that a few times to build up a whistling-good speed and squeezed the roan forward. The knot landed solid enough it should've raised a welt even through her tough hide—I never bothered to look—and she bolted back into the herd, which by now had prudently moved away from the battleground.

"On watch, Beggar," I told him and waved him toward the sheep. He looked kinda resentful when I did that, but I think the old devil was play-acting to save his pride in public. After all, there *was* a stranger watching. Or at least a nonfamily member. He went trotting back to the sheep and took up his duties with animals he knew how to handle. And that showed proper respect for a herd dog.

The red bull calf had long since disappeared. I checked and saw he'd found his mama all right and was tucked in close to her flank like he'd been pasted there. The cow was too worked up by now to be messed with. She might've turned on the horse, and the rider, if I tried to fool with her now so I went and found me another calf to take to the fire. That one little fellow could wait a bit longer.

CHAPTER 23

Brock rode in that evening. He was by himself, and his horse looked fresh and little used. I was willing to bet he had not gone with Herring all the way to town and back that day but had broken away early and spent his time somewhere nearer, maybe up on the hill watching us at work.

He didn't speak a greeting to me when he rode into the yard, just swung off his horse and tied it to one of the uprights Reese had set firmly into the ground when he built his pens. Judging from the look on Brock's face I was glad Amanda was up at the house preparing our dinner. Somehow I didn't think I would need to ask her to set another place.

"You've come to some sort of decision," I said when Brock was done fooling with his horse and turned to face me. I couldn't help but notice that the thong had been slipped off his revolver hammer.

He nodded.

"You're going to try me."

He took in a long breath but again he nodded.

"I wish you wouldn't do that, Richard." And I meant it sincerely. I believe he knew that.

"This has gone too far, Priest. You have to go," he said.

"Things are getting rough now? On you, I mean?"

Brock gave me a look that had pain in it and I believe a hint of embarrassment as well. He nodded. He spread his hands apologetically. "Look, Priest . . . Jude . . ." He almost smiled. "It seems kind of odd to be calling you that now."

"I think we've come to know each other fairly well, Richard. Everything considered. I'd even admit that I like you."

This time he did smile. "You're a sonuvabitch, Judas Priest. You just don't make this any easier."

"Tell me about it, Richard."

He thought it over for a moment and gave me a shrug that said why-not as completely as words could have done. He had already determined that one of us was not going to be alive tomorrow to care.

"You know the Association is having its troubles."

I nodded.

"The die-up hurt, cut the membership, cut the income. I told you all that. And there's politics involved, causing some bad feelings among those that are left and still reasonably healthy at the banks." He sighed. "It's been kind of a bad time all around. Greenough isn't helping it any. He's coming out as a power these days and he wants a lot more than he already has. Before . . . he wasn't such a big fish. He's taking this as his chance to move up and out. He wants more than just money here. He wants to be able to show the other members that he has a handle on things in Wyoming, that he's the one they should count on to pull it all back together. If he can keep sheep off the Thunder Basin grass he can use that as a flag, rally some of the other boys around him if you know what I mean."

I told him I did.

"Right, well, he's determined as hell about this. In the old days, before the die-up, he probably would have hired an army of people to come up here and blow you off the range. Right now he can't do that. He doesn't have all that much money right now and the Association doesn't either, to tell you the truth. Besides, he wants this to be all his own show. It has to be all his if he wants those other boys to back him, look up to him as the leader. Without something to show them he can't pull them all in behind him. The regular leadership . . . they don't support him all that much. He has to have this first, then maybe he can throw his weight around, see?"

I grunted to let him know I was following him.

Brock's expression twisted, really looked painful now. "I . . . don't like the way he's going about this, Jude. I swear I don't. Greenough has brought in . . . a specialist. Not connected with the Association at all. It isn't . . . right, dammit. It isn't right at all. I don't want . . . someone else to settle this. Do you understand that?"

"I think so. I thank you for it, Richard."

He bobbed his head unhappily. "This should have been done between you and me. And the law. The way a man can hold his head up. You know?"

"I know. Tell me something, Richard."

"Yeah?"

"You've been having your doubts. Not just about Greenough but the Association too. Why've you stayed with them when you could have gone somewhere else, someplace you could have liked better?"

His answering smile was bitter. "They pay awfully well."

"There's more to it than that, Richard."

"I take their pay, though."

"You don't need it that badly. Nobody does."

"No. I guess not." He shook his head quickly. He looked angry. "I've been with the Association a good, long time now. Started with them when I wasn't much more than a kid. A little wild maybe. Not much judgment then."

"A little too wild, Richard?"

He smiled a sad, bitter smile. "A little too wild. I did . . . something. Not exactly on orders. In excess of orders, you might say. It was a while ago. But there are people who remember it. I remember it myself. Too damned often, I do. It wasn't pretty. I'm not proud of it. But I did it. I have to live with it."

"And if you ever decide to bolt the organization there might be someone who would remember that? Maybe let it be known in the wrong places?" I asked. "Like maybe Greenough?"

He nodded unhappily. "Like maybe Greenough. He, uh, mentioned it to me when I was down in Cheyenne." He looked me in the eye for the first time since he had begun talking. "I have family near Fort Laramie. They're good people, Jude." He smiled. "Not like you and me, huh? But they really are. They wouldn't understand. It isn't like it would come to a trial or anything. I know that wouldn't happen. The Association wouldn't let it happen. But my folks knowing about it." He shook his head. "I couldn't hurt them like that."

I understood. Maybe better than he realized. I'd hurt my own people that way and even the change of name hadn't kept them from feeling the sting of it or me from feeling the guilt of doing it. It was too late now for me to change anything, too late by a long ways, but I could understand Brock's reluctance to do the same thing. If I had taken the time to think about that the time I had the fight with the old man maybe I would have done things differently myself. Brock still had the chance to avoid my mistake. But one of us was going to have to die because of his opportunity.

Brock looked down for a moment but forced himself to meet my eyes again and squared his shoulders before he spoke. "I hope you know, Jude, that I want to do this myself because . . . I want it done . . . properly, if you know what I mean. I don't want it to be some stranger who doesn't know or care about anything but his pay. And I *do* really believe you're wrong to be bringing sheep onto this grass."

"I know that, Richard. I don't think you'd be here if you didn't believe that."

He looked genuinely relieved. He smiled. "You know, those penny dreadfuls print a lot of trash about standup fights. I don't think I ever heard of an honest-to-God one before."

"By damn, Richard, I never did either."

Pretty soon the both of us were standing there laughing to beat all billy hell, amused by the silly sight we must have made, squared off and liking each other and about to actually do something as stupid as shoot at somebody we really liked and know we were going to be shot back at if the other one could.

And I don't believe Brock had any doubt that he was going to kill me, no more than I had any real doubt that I was going to kill him.

You just can't go into a gunfight if you don't believe you are going to win it.

Both of us were old enough and had seen enough to know that we neither one was thunder and lightning. We neither one of us had any of the old Indian superstitions about amulets that could turn bullets or anything like that. We both knew that someday we would go under. But like all men we believed that that time would come a long way in the future when we were gray-headed and crochety and ready for it. Certainly not this fine evening with the air so soft and pleasantly cool and Amanda Reese's beeves grazing out on the grass behind Richard, and Howard Blackburn's sheep snuffling around in the dirt of the big pen and making their low, soothing, blatting noises. We neither one of us really believed right then that it could actually happen to him.

"Just a minute then, Richard," I said when we were done laughing and finally sobered to what lay before us.

I whistled Beggar to heel and took him into the big, log-walled barn. I ordered him to sit-stay and closed the door on him so he couldn't get out to join in and protect me, either way it went.

"Thank you, Jude," Richard said when I came out alone.

"Sure."

"How are we supposed to do this anyway? Who goes first?"

"I don't guess either wants to do that," I admitted.

"We need a signal of some sort."

I grinned. "If anybody could hear us I'll bet it would sound like a couple kids playing in the schoolyard after hours."

"But it isn't," he said seriously.

"No. It isn't."

"Is the dog likely to bark?"

"No."

He paused, looked thoughtful for a moment. "Can anyone else handle him? The woman maybe?"

"No. No chance."

"I'm sorry, but I'll probably have to shoot him then. Put him down quick for you. I won't make it painful."

"No. You won't have to worry about that, Richard." Oddly enough I felt myself getting mad then. I certainly hadn't been before. And I guess it showed well enough for he started to get mad then too. I guess it was the excuse we were needing.

Brock's voice was cold when he said, "On three then." And he started to count.

The both of us waited to the last sound of the last number, and it was over just that soon. With only the one shot fired. It took him in the chest and brought a look of sudden surprise to his face, and I took no pleasure in seeing it there.

He might still have gotten a shot off as he went down, but he was done and I believe he knew it even before he was through, and he made no attempt to bring his Colt the rest of the way up and trigger it. He was good enough to have done it, I know, and he was very nearly fast enough, but he did not try and I was still liking him when he died.

CHAPTER 24

"Where are you going?" she mumbled in a soft voice.

I wanted to kiss her and stroke her hair—so smooth and fine even cut as short as it was—but I could not no matter how strong the temptation of this woman. "The dog and me'd better get on out to the barn now. If somebody comes messing around the sheep I want to be there." I'd gotten in the habit of spending the after-supper hours in that easy chair with her near me, and I wished I could do it still. Lord, but I was coming to think a lot of this woman. She brought to me a kind of peaceful comfort I had never known before.

"Is it because of me, Jude?"

I stood and took my gunbelt from the peg and buckled it in place. I'd been wearing it so long I wouldn't have felt comfortable without it even if there wouldn't be a need to have it there. I sat down again and touched her lightly. "That would be something to consider, sure. Anyplace I might have to shoot from would be shot back at, it's true, and I wouldn't want to have any fire coming your way. But mostly I got to be out there because I can't hear so good or react as quick from inside. Even ol' Beggar couldn't hear or smell as well if he was cooped up inside. All right?"

I could feel the tension subside from her. "All right, Jude. Whatever you think best."

"Not that I like it, mind. I'd rather be with you."

"Good!" she said firmly. She surprised me. And pleased me. It was—I hoped—an indication that maybe she, too, felt something of what I had come to feel toward her.

"Get a good sleep, woman." I touched her shoulder and made my way slowly to the front door and out into the night air. It was too dark to see him but I could hear and could feel Beggar moving with me. "Good boy," I told him.

The night air was cool enough to almost be chilly. I shivered but

I was liking it, fresh and clean and smelling like spring water tastes.

I could hear the woollies shifting around in the pen a little though most of them would've been asleep. They weren't excited about anything anyway.

The barn was dark but I didn't want to show a light. Besides, it wasn't really necessary. I had left my gear just inside the door. I found the shotgun by feel and transferred a fistful of shells from my warbag to my pockets. I hadn't planned on taking my bedroll but decided that as cool as it was I'd better add that to the load.

I felt my way around the pen and didn't stumble over roots or rocks or whatever more than a half dozen times. Beggar didn't seem to be having that problem, darn him.

There was a nice flat area just below and on the far side of the big pen that seemed not to have too much rock in the soil. With my luck it would turn out to be where Reese had had a manure pile but I figured it would be the best I could find in the dark and spread my bedroll there. It was cool enough to feel good under the cover, and I let Beggar crawl in beside me for company. I don't often do that but he always likes it when he's allowed.

With Beggar and me both being light sleepers I felt safe enough to doze. I wasn't really expecting trouble so soon after Brock's visit anyway.

Which just shows what can happen when you think you can outsmart the other guy.

Sometime during the night I woke to the sound of a bullet thumping into wood. Beggar and I both came up from under the canvas and were wide awake before we could hear the sound of the shot. It came from out on the grass somewhere.

It had to be from a long way out. There was quite a lag between the strike of the bullet and the sound of the shot. And Beggar hadn't been disturbed any more than I was beforehand.

Some sorry sonuvabitch out there in the night was throwing lead in the general direction of the 2R headquarters in the hope of maybe hitting a sheep or a horse. Or a human. It was a lousy thing to do. He was risking hitting Manda on the slimmest chance he might also kill a two-dollar wether.

The worst part of it was that I couldn't do a thing to stop him. I couldn't see to shoot at him, and if I could have, the shotgun would've been as much good as a handful of pebbles. I couldn't chase after him for that would leave the place open to raiders who might be waiting for just such a chance. All I could do was to calm Beggar and hide behind something. I stayed put and stayed quiet, but, Lord God, I did cuss that man inside my head.

The muzzle flash bloomed out on the grass. It looked nearly half a mile out. The bullet sizzled past somewhere off to the right, missing the buildings completely, and smacked into the ground or maybe the hillside somewhere there. It seemed a long time before I heard the shot.

Another muzzle flash followed. Judging from the amount of time between shots he was using a long-range smokepole like mine was and not some short and stubby saddlegun like a working cowboy would carry. This shot sounded like it hit the barn. The sheep began waking and getting restless.

"Jude? *Jude!*" The front door slammed and I could hear her run into the yard. The rifleman fired again.

"Stay, Beggar. Guard." I took off toward her.

There was some thin brush growing below the pen and I think I ran into every scrap of it in the dark. "Get in the house, Manda. Get back."

A bullet went by with its short, ugly thup of sound, and this time the sound of the strike had that dull, wet quality to it that came from hitting meat. A sheep grunted out a too-short bleat.

"Get back, Manda, damn you."

The fence railing finally ended—it had never seemed so big—and I stumbled onto the open yard.

"Jude?" She wasn't twenty yards away. My eyes had adjusted to the dark more than I'd realized. I could see a dim shape moving toward me.

I grabbed her up and dragged her with me and ran for the barn. I heard a bullet shatter glass. That one must have hit the house. It could have hit Manda too.

We lay panting in the dirt of the barn floor and I held her near. "Are you all right? You aren't hurt?"

"Just the bruises from you throwing me around." She was laughing about it. Some miserable bastard was out there in the dark shooting at us, and she was still able to laugh. "What about you?"

"Fine. Just worried. About you."

Another bullet hit the barn. It sounded almost distant with the noise of the strike coming through the thickness of the log walls. We were safe enough in here.

I sat her up and tried to brush the dirt from her clothes and found she wasn't wearing much in that category. "Oh. Sorry." She laughed again.

I heard the sound of the rifle again. I hadn't heard where that bullet went.

"Shouldn't you bring the dog in?"

"No. If anybody comes near he'll know it first. He needs to be where he can hear and smell."

"What if he's hurt?"

"Someone will be very sorry." There seemed no point in telling her someone already would be very sorry. I'd been upset with Lawrence Greenough before but not really with Brock or any of the LG crew. Whatever I'd done was only what I had to do. Now I guess I was mad. They had shot at Manda. At least where she could be hurt if not directly at her. I did not like that. Somebody was going to know that sooner or later. Somebody who carried a long-barreled, slow-loading rifle.

Manda moved closer against me and I held her as she seemed to want. She touched my face and raised her lips to mine. The touch, her kiss, were enough to dizzy me and make it almost worthwhile to be shot at. I believe she wanted to soothe as much as to be soothed.

We lay in the barn and waited out the firing. Or I did. She fell asleep, somehow, during it.

He fired forty rounds in all. I was sure of the count. Two cartons of cartridges. He would reload them now. Have them ready to use again at his leisure. I heard nothing more after that and eventually called Beggar in to keep watch beside us. I could have wakened the woman. Maybe I should have. She certainly would've slept better inside. But I needed to stay out and I wanted her near. I suppose I could have told myself that the rifleman might have a third carton of cartridges. The truth was that I wanted her near me the rest of this night.

So Beggar and I sat on the earth in the doorway, close enough that I could hear the slow, soft rhythm of her breath in sleep, and waited for the dawn.

CHAPTER 25

"Are you sure it's safe to just . . . act normal?"

"Uh huh." I finished pulling the front cinch snug and gave it an extra tug for good measure. The back cinch I secured loose under the sorrel's belly. A flank cinch is really needed just for roping but I wouldn't be comfortable with one of those center-fire single-cinch saddles popular up North here. "He won't be there now." I could've been wrong but I couldn't see any sense in telling her that.

"You do like I told you, Manda. Fix us a good breakfast while I look around a bit. And don't worry. There shouldn't be any trouble now."

I could see that she didn't like it, but she didn't argue with me. I liked that about her, too. Among other things.

"And don't worry if I seem to act a little strange now. I'm just making sure I'm right. You wait just a minute an' then go on up to the house."

I gave her a kiss that I'd intended to be quick but it lingered a while without making me angry. I let go of her finally and stepped onto the sorrel, right there inside the barn. We hadn't showed ourselves outside yet and I figured the first look might as well be a sudden one, just in case the guy did have that third box of shells.

The roof was low and I had to sit the horse bent over just to keep from braining myself while the sorrel was standing quiet. I took an extra moment to hope he'd not rear, clucked once to Beggar and threw the steel to the horse. The sorrel didn't rear but he sure did jump.

I went kiting out of there like a drunk on his way to a dance and Beggar right behind, running as hard as he could. We must've made a real stirring sight.

The performance was wasted. Nobody shot at me. Well, I hadn't expected anyone to. I couldn't say I was disappointed.

I reined the sorrel down after the first mad dash and circled back to the pen. The sheep were calm and peaceful. There were two dirty, trampled carcasses in the dirt. All that fuss and all he'd done was kill two sheep out of the thousand in the big pen. He'd shot up near their value in the powder and lead it took to kill them.

I hadn't come out here to look at dead woollies, though. I'd seen some of those before. Beggar took his signal and loped out onto the grass ahead of me with his head high and nostrils open to the scents around him. I knew about where to look, but it was the dog that found the exact spot. There wasn't really anything special to mark it except maybe the scent the rifleman left there. I swung down from the horse and stood looking back at the buildings.

From here in daylight one good man with a rifle could really smoke up the place, and I was glad it was such a different story in the dark, with the hill behind to make sure there wasn't even an outline to aim at.

I don't know what, if anything, I'd been hoping to find out here. Whatever it was I didn't find it. He hadn't dropped an empty casing to tell me about his rifle, and if he'd done any smoking he had carried his butts or stubs or dottle away with him. I couldn't even find where he had staked his horse although he had to have had one with him. No one was likely to be fool enough to trust someone else to pick him up. Not when they couldn't be sure that I wouldn't come out after them. Or him.

Beggar was getting bored with this and so was I. I got back onto the horse and headed in. By the time I finished the morning chores Manda should have breakfast ready.

She did, and it was a good one. She waited until we were done eating before she asked, "Will they do it again?"

"Likely yes. If he's smart he'll try to catch me laying for him the next time. If I'm smart I won't let him."

She frowned. "You're so matter-of-fact about this, Jude. It scares me."

"You didn't act it last night. And me, I've been there before." I grinned. "It's a funny thing, but people can get used to 'most anything, even the idea that there are people around who want to kill you. This fella, shoot, he hasn't done anything so far but be a little annoying. But look here, woman, there's worse to come. If I stay here. I've been thinking it would be better for me to take my sheep somewhere else."

"No!" Her answer came spitting out fast and firm.

"Uh-uh. Don't be answering so quick, dammit. That's something you need to think on for a minute first. It's only sensible that I go."

"If you want me to think about it I will. But the answer will be the same."

"That reaction is pure emotion, woman. I appreciate it, but it isn't sensible. Being here I just draw their fire."

"Then *you* be sensible, Jude. This is the only patented grass in the whole territory you can use without getting jailed for trespass, and Greenough still has that order saying you can't use public grass. It will take weeks, maybe months to get a federal judge to set it aside. If you leave here you have to head for Dakota, and Greenough would win, at least for now.

"Aside from your sheep business, I need your help here with my cows. I don't intend to lose them. You're helping me work them. More than that you are helping keep Greenough occupied with a worry bigger than my cows and grass. You're helping me just by being in the territory. And that is quite apart from the other reasons I want you to stay here."

I shook my head. "Too dangerous."

"Dangerous, hell," she said disgustedly. "There's no bullet going to come through these log walls. If I hadn't gotten scared and run outside last night I could have slept in my own bed and never worried about a thing."

I didn't have to say anything to knock that theory. I just turned my head and gave a pointed look toward the broken glass on the living-room floor where a bullet had hit.

She waved a hand in dismissal of that worry. "I didn't have the shutters closed. From now on I'll latch them at night."

"It's just too dangerous for you, Manda."

"If you leave you're running out on me and your employer too, Jude. I don't think you'd do that. Besides, what makes you think the LG would quit shooting just because you left? My being here didn't stop them last night. If something happened to me by 'accident' it could save Greenough a lot of court expenses. I might need your help with or without those smelly sheep being here."

I hadn't thought of that, but I had to admit it was a possibility. Whoever had done that shooting during the night sure didn't seem to fret much about there being a woman in the house.

"We'll see," I told her, but if I left, it was clear I would have to take her to Dakota with me just to keep her safe. If I did that it would mean everybody would lose, her and Blackburn and me. Everybody but Lawrence Greenough and his LG outfit.

Oddly enough I never even gave a thought then to what carrying her with me would mean in terms of being responsible for her. I'd never been responsible for another human person. A dog or two and some livestock was all I'd ever been willing to watch over. Now it just seemed kind of natural that I would be thinking of her future too.

"We'll see," I repeated, more to myself than to her.

She gave me a quiet little bit of a smile and began clearing the dishes away. She poured me a fresh cup of coffee and went to sweep up the broken glass from the floor.

"Manda."

"Yes?"

"I wish we knew for sure if you're a widow."

"I am. Count on it."

But the truth is that I was afraid to. She'd already told me, and no beating around the bush to it, if her man showed up alive she still belonged to him. By choice. I began hoping he was dead. I take no pride in that but it was so.

Later on I saddled a horse for her and she helped drag the dead sheep a ways down the hillside so I could bury them. It was a lot of extra work when the coyotes and other scavengers would have cleaned them up in a few days, but I don't like to leave dead woollies out where they can give predators a taste for their meat. It's safer to keep such vermin used to catching rabbits or mice for their eating, and I figured old Beggar had all the troubles he needed without me adding more in that way.

"We'll not be branding calves today if you don't mind," I told her when I was done with my shovel work.

"There aren't many left anyway. They can wait a while."

"Good. Beggar and me can take the flock out in the open, and I'll catch some sleep while he keeps watch. If you see or hear anything fire your rifle. I won't go so far he can't hear it."

"All right. I need to do some work in the garden anyway and gather some eggs. The hens hide them pretty well." She smiled. "And I believe I promised to do some baking for you. Now go tend your sheep. I have things to do."

We parted in the ranch yard, she heading for the house and me working with Beggar to put the wethers out on the grass way past the time when they should've been grazing. The only thing that marked this one as different from a normal day of herding was that I was riding now with the long-barreled rifle in my hand instead of under my leg, where it usually hung. That was different. And so was my anticipation of coming in in the evening. I almost had the feeling then of going home after the day's work.

CHAPTER 26

We were playing a game of cat and mouse that would have been childish if it hadn't been deadly.

Whoever this rifleman was, he was good. He worked alone and at long range, never coming in close where I could get to him and never allowing himself a pattern that would have let me lay for him in the dark and take him with the shotgun. Which I would have done without qualm No. 1 if I'd had the chance. This stuff about the honor involved in a standup fight is just so much bunk. And I'd had a bellyful of that with Brock. Him at least I had liked. This fellow had come for me in the dark, and I would take him any time and any way I could.

The trouble was that I couldn't.

With just me to defend the place against a possible raid by the whole LG crew I couldn't range very far from the house, and our friendly neighborhood rifleman refused to come in close.

I did try moving out as far as I thought I dared and lying in ambush across routes I thought he might use, but it did no good. Only once did I even get close enough to the man that Beggar could let me know when he was coming to his stand, which he changed each and every night. He never used the same one twice, either. Never went back to one.

Sometime during the night, though, we could count on him opening up and firing his forty shots. He never shot more and never less. Forty shots and he was gone.

It was tempting to let him start shooting and then head out for him. But I think that would've been a mistake and maybe a fatal one. Any man as careful as he was about not setting up regular habits in other ways wasn't going to fall into that pattern by accident. That one was so plain to see that I was leery of it. It could be he was counting on exactly that, but I wasn't going to bank on it. So I stayed put and waited close to the house and pens.

Manda adjusted just fine, or at least she seemed to. After supper we'd close and bolt the shutters and read or something until I figured it was time to go out and wait for our rifleman. She'd blow out the lights then and go to bed, and after a few nights she claimed she'd never been so well rested from such early bedtimes. She said she woke up while he was shooting but was able to sleep the rest of the time.

We lost three more sheep to the random shooting, and one of Manda's horses was shot in the neck but not bad enough to put him down. I cut some heavy brush and piled it against the fences, which seemed to help. The leaves and smaller branches also gave the wethers something they weren't supposed to eat but did anyway.

During the days we grazed the sheep and found enough time between naps (mine; Manda didn't need any) to finish branding the half dozen or so calves she hadn't found in those first couple gathers.

The shooting went on for five more nights and on the sixth we had silence the whole night through. Damned if that wasn't more unnerving by then than the shooting would have been. I kept expecting something to happen and nothing did.

It was all a matter of guess and wait, anyway, and no way to tell who was winning. I couldn't do anything to get him, yet whatever cute tricks he was planning I wasn't biting. I never once so much as fired back when he was shooting. And now he didn't seem to be shooting anymore. I did have to wonder what he would be up to next. Well, he was probably wondering what I'd been up to too. That wasn't much of anything, really, but *he* wouldn't know that.

Along about nine o'clock of the morning following that first sleep-through night I saw two horsemen coming down from the north. They were riding in plain sight and as I'd kept the flock in not far from the buildings—still being worried about what the fella was up to—I had time to put them back into the big pen before the riders arrived. By then I'd identified one of them as Sheriff Herring. The other I hadn't seen before.

We met them at the front door of the house, and I had the shotgun in my hands. I'd set the far-reaching gun inside as I didn't figure to need any weapon and figured if I did it would be close-range work. Since it was her place I kind of stepped aside and let Manda do the greeting.

She was cordial enough, more than I would've been under the circumstances, and invited them in for coffee.

The two men left their horses and brushed the dust of riding from their britches. Arlo touched his hat to Manda and nodded to me.

"Good morning, Mrs. Reese. Priest." He tilted his head toward the tall, thin, consumptive-looking man beside him and said, "This is Orval Hatcher. He, uh, asked if he could come along today."

Manda said something polite about the coffee being ready soon and they should sit and be comfortable. I wasn't really listening to what-all she was saying.

Back behind her I was taking a long look at Orval Hatcher. Val to his friends and to those too scared to admit they weren't his friends. This was our rifleman. He'd come to pay us a call.

Judging from the way Arlo Herring was acting the name Val Hatcher didn't seem to mean anything up here, but I had sure heard of him down home. I hadn't heard the name since I left Texas a dozen years before but even then he was known if not respected.

I looked him over good. The man was holding his age fairly well. He had to be in his late forties at the least and probably was across the line into fifty-some. There wasn't much gray in his hair, and he was dressed like a timber surveyor or some such respectable profession. Lace-up high boots outside his britches with a neat roll of knitted stockings showing at the top. Comfortable-looking sweater over a flannel shirt with a tie knotted at the throat. He was wearing a narrow-brimmed hat. And no gun that I could see.

He was clean-shaven and might've been decent-looking if he didn't have that thin, pale, undernourished look of consumption. He really did not look at all like what he was.

What the man was was a professional killer, plain and simple, and the fact that he'd been able to avoid a nickname like Hatchet or something comparable with his own being Hatcher was a testimonial to how good he was and how much people were scared of him.

Way back when I'd been hearing of him they said his fee was high, several hundred dollars for a white man. What it would be now I had no way of knowing. But they said he guaranteed his work. No performance, no pay.

He'd been known then as a loner, with a telegraph address in San

Antonio and a lot of work in Mexico. He hadn't been famous, exactly. Not the way Sam Bass was or John Hardin and Ben Thompson were. But Hatcher was talked about.

I hadn't heard anything about him in years but it looked like he was still doing business as usual.

He was looking me over as carefully as I was inspecting him. I doubted, though, that he had ever heard of me. When I was in Texas it was as a kid and by a different name at that. Judas Priest was known a lot of miles and a couple mountain chains away from Val Hatcher's home territory. Certainly I hadn't heard of Hatcher in years, and my name would not be carried as far or as often as his. Nor in the same circles. I tried to look as meek and inoffensive as I reasonably could. If he wanted to underrate the opposition it was all right by me.

Manda showed us all to the table and seemed mildly curious but not upset when I maneuvered the sheriff slightly so that Hatcher ended up sitting next to me.

"Now, Arlo, what was it you wanted?" Manda asked lightly as she poured fresh water from a bucket into the big pot. She set it on the stove and built the fire higher.

Herring seemed nervous. He went to shove his hat back and pushed his finger into empty air in the neighborhood of his forehead. He'd left his hat and gunbelt at the door again. The man really looked uncomfortable.

"Well, ma'am, I'm supposed to tell you a hearing's been scheduled before Judge Wilder on Thursday. First thing in the morning, ma'am."

"What day is this, Arlo?"

"Monday, ma'am. The first of the week."

"Thank you, Arlo. We tend to lose track of the days here." She sighed and sat to wait for her water to boil. "I take it the witness got here then?"

"Well . . . yes. Last night." The sheriff still seemed uneasy, maybe embarrassed.

"They didn't waste any time then," Manda said.

"No, ma'am. The judge met with them last night. They got me out of bed to tell me. I started down right away so you'd have as much time as possible to prepare."

"Why, thank you, Arlo." She looked questioningly toward Hatcher.

The killer smiled. When he spoke his voice was gentle, his tone almost courtly. "I insisted the sheriff bring me along, Mrs. Reese. I hadn't known the extent of this misunderstanding until I arrived here, nor its effect." His smile was warm and really quite charming. "I wouldn't want to face you for the first time in a courtroom, Mrs. Reese. That would be too impersonal. And very unfair to you. I want to assure you, ma'am, here and now, that I will tell the court only the simple truth."

"*You* are the witness?" She sounded disbelieving, as well she might. Even without knowing what I did of the man his presence here would have seemed a rude and unnecessary thing.

"Yes, ma'am," Hatcher said politely. "I was present at the transaction. It took place over in Dakota Territory. I happened to be there looking to fill a contract for railroad ties. I was having a drink with Mr. Pyle when the agreement was reached and a bank draft given. On an Omaha bank. I remember that in particular because I've had occasion to do railroad business—and personal business as well, I might add—at the same bank." He sounded disarmingly sincere. Any jury in the world would believe him from his manner alone. He probably could've convinced them he'd seen Lincoln playing poker with John W. Booth the day *after* the President was shot. The man might have made his fortune better as an actor than an assassin.

It was clear Manda didn't know what to say or do. The sonuvabitch was so convincing it looked like *she* believed him.

"Somehow, sheriff," I cut in, "I got the idea this witness for the LG was one of their own hands that they couldn't find right off. Fella that used to work for them."

"I told you that all right, son. That was the understanding I had at the time. I was mistaken, that's all."

"Uh huh," I said. And I did understand. Hatcher couldn't pose as a former LG hand without somebody wondering why he'd never been seen around here before. Somebody had thought of that after the game was already started. Or Greenough found himself needing a gunhand too and decided to get double duty out of his fee to Hatcher by having the one man do both jobs.

I would've been willing to bet that somewhere there was an unhappy cowboy who'd been promised a windfall and then had it pulled back out of reach. If Manda could've found him and persuaded him to talk it sure could help her. One thing was sure, though. Lawrence Greenough couldn't have found any cowboy anywhere who could play the witness better than Val Hatcher was doing. Hell, he couldn't have found anybody better for the part if he'd gone to New York and hired somebody off a stage to do it.

Manda was really upset by Hatcher's presence, and she only knew half or maybe a quarter of the story on the man. I swear she seemed to be believing him herself, and she knew the whole thing to be a lie.

She came to her feet and I could see that she was clutching the material in the skirt part of her dress. Her hands like that looked lined and wrinkled and older than she was.

"Please. Excuse me," she blurted. She turned and fled into the bedroom.

"You've had a long ride, I know," I said, "but . . ."

"Of course." Herring came to his feet. His look was apologetic. "I thought it only right that she know at once. It must be an awful shock." The sheriff believed the man's story then, and I can't believe he was any part of the deal. At this point he seemed genuinely convinced that the LG had bought and paid for Manda Reese's cows.

Val Hatcher stood too, very much the polite and proper gentleman. He even managed to look vaguely sympathetic when he extended his hand to a man he was here to kill, after he'd just finished lying to a woman he intended to help rob and ruin.

Well, I've never had any trouble keeping my feelings to myself and I didn't have any now. I took his hand and shook it and thanked him for coming in person to tell us. I smiled at him and thought how I wouldn't at all mind grassing this gentleman and paying him back for Lord knows how many dead and buried men. Or women too, for that matter. There wasn't much I would put beneath this fellow.

I followed them out to their horses and smiled and thanked them both again for their kindness, and when I casually leaned my hand on the rump of Val Hatcher's horse I put it beside the polished wood of a curly-grained rifle stock concealed there in a long, leather boot. I was looking into Hatcher's eyes when I did it, and the man never flinched. He smiled like it was a great joke on this unsuspecting sheepherder to be that close to touching the very gun that had been spitting so much lead at me. And at Manda. He seemed to think the whole thing great fun. Well let him have his fun now, I figured.

I'd have mine later.

CHAPTER 27

"Are you all right, Manda?" That was just the routine, meaningless sort of thing a person asks at such times, though. It didn't mean anything really. It was plain to see that she was not all right.

She was standing at the front-facing bedroom window, watching the sheriff and the rifleman ride away. At least looking dully in their direction. I doubt she was seeing them much. She was too much woman to get that panicky, stricken look about her that some females turn to when they're upset, but she did look kind of lost and alone there. I guess the props had pretty much been knocked clean out from under her world. All the faith she had put in her man would now seem to her to have been misplaced.

I went to her and took her by the shoulders and pulled her back to sit on the edge of the bed. She didn't look at me and I guessed that it wasn't pride but a sense of forlorn unworthiness that kept her from turning to me now.

"It isn't at all what you think, Manda. Look at me a minute. Manda!" I reached out and turned her head toward me. "Manda. Listen to me. I want to tell you about Val Hatcher."

I did, and her eyes, at first dulled by deep hurt, began to come alive with interest and with dawning realization and finally with a hot, fierce hatred for the man who had so coolly set about destroying her pride and the very foundations of her knowledge of self-worth.

"Are you sure, Jude?" she asked finally.

I nodded. I told her about the rifle in the long, slim scabbard on his saddle and the laughter in his eyes when I stood so near and so apparently unsuspecting.

"Do you *know* what I was thinking?"

"I believe so, Manda. And some of what you would've been feeling. You couldn't have thought or felt otherwise if he was telling the truth. But he wasn't."

She began to look thoughtful then as well as angry. "He had me fooled, Jude. He had Arlo fooled. Still does. He'll do the same with the court, even if I demand a jury trial."

"Uh huh. He's good at telling his tale. Even you believed it. But now you know different. Whatever else happens, whatever a court might decide, *you* know different."

She put her cheek against my chest and leaned against me. "Thank you, Jude." After a time she sat upright again and looked at me closely. "Jude! Arlo was here and you never said the first word about the shooting, about what that pig Hatcher has been doing out here nights."

I grinned at her. "Nope. Not a word."

"But why?"

"Well, honey, I think the sheriff is a pretty good man. Even if it is Association business, he might want to help. He might go so far as to send a man out here to stand watch with us. We wouldn't want that now, would we?"

She tossed her head indignantly. "I certainly don't see why we wouldn't."

"It could be somebody who'd get in the way, maybe somebody who'd rather get in the way than help, honey."

"I wish you wouldn't call me that. And it wouldn't hurt you to be a little more trusting of people."

"That's just the point. It *could* hurt to be too trusting. I might not always be right, but I'm still alive. That counts for something. Is that what he called you?"

"Who . . . oh, yes. I hope you don't mind, but . . ."

"No, it's okay, Manda. Sorry." But I did feel a little awkward now. It wasn't the reminder of her feelings toward the dead husband although maybe I was a little bit jealous of that too. There was no sense in letting that get to me, though. She'd had a good marriage with the guy. She was a lot of woman and all of it had been his. Now . . . I didn't know.

And I guess that was what was really bothering me. We had said a few things to each other and maybe even were becoming something to each other, but she had never once offered to make any commitments to or for me. She hadn't made any claims on me either, it was true, but I wasn't really appreciating that fact like I might have. Her turning aside my use of a pet name for her kind of said she was satisfied with the way things were now and that she wouldn't be interested in changing any of it.

I could have been happy about that. I suppose. My life had been well ordered for a long time. For some reason I wasn't all that pleased. And I sure wasn't looking forward to this job ending, no matter what happened with Lawrence Greenough and his LG outfit.

"If you aren't going to ask Arlo for help, what are we going to do, Jude? Just let that man keep shooting all night every night?"

It took me a moment to return to the train of thought we'd been on before I got sidetracked in my private thinking. "Huh? Oh, no. Not exactly. I know a little more about him now. Besides, I don't think he'll be doing that so much now."

Her eyebrows went up.

"Whatever he was trying to accomplish with that wasn't working. I still don't know what all he might've had in mind but if it was working he'd have stayed with it. That's why he didn't come last night. He got his sleep in and then rode in to Wolf Creek to put in a public appearance and start your part of it going. There might not be another person in the territory who knows he's been here a week already. And we couldn't prove it. Neither of us actually saw him."

Manda shuddered. "I should *say* I didn't. I wouldn't want to."

"Oh-h-h-h-h I would," I said softly. "I sure do hope I'll see the gentleman again soon."

I must have been showing more than I intended of what I felt about Val Hatcher, for Manda said, "I wish you wouldn't talk like that, Jude. And you have that . . . look . . . that I don't like. If I didn't know you, Jude, I swear I'd be afraid of you when you're like this."

I got myself in hand better and gave her a nice, normal kind of smile. "You don't ever have to be scared of me, Manda. I can promise you that."

"You don't make promises lightly, do you?"

"No."

She smiled back and a tension in her that I hadn't really noticed before seemed to flow out of her and away now. She came back to me and relaxed in my arms. It felt good to have her there.

"You sure do tempt a man to ignore his work."

She giggled. "Good." She turned her face up to be kissed and I enjoyed it more than I had any right to.

"Umm. I can't think of a better reason to stay, but I'll bet those woollies are hungry."

"If I can't convince you to stay maybe I can get you to take me along. There isn't anyone around for miles and miles. And you don't have much to do out there all by yourself."

"Now that sounds like the nicest suggestion I've heard in a long time. Get your clothes changed if you need to. I'll saddle a horse for you."

"All right. And Jude?"

"Uh huh."

"Thank you. For everything."

"It's my pleasure, Manda. It really is." I got out of there and headed for the barn before I got to saying things that might be more than she wanted to hear.

Val Hatcher would probably be tied up in town for a day or two, but I wasn't going to count on that. About the time I did I might find myself guessing wrong, and that could be bad. Howard Blackburn stood to lose some sheep if that happened. Amanda Reese could lose a whole lot more than that.

We ate an early supper and I was down in the barn with Beggar and the shotgun by dark.

Manda had sent out a stoppered gourd filled with hot coffee and wrapped in a towel to help keep it warm. She'd wanted to come herself but I wouldn't let her. I was tired and would have enough trouble staying awake and alert without having her there to distract my attention. Though I would have liked it.

Beggar and I were getting to be old hands at this night-watch business, and the bottle of hot coffee made it almost pleasant. That was a fine idea she'd had and one I would use again.

I stationed the dog below the big pen and took my place at the barn door so I could be close to both the sheep and the house. The LG seemed to have Manda's whole herd pretty much in their hands already but I wasn't going to count on them being willing to leave it at that. If nothing else they might realize they could get at me through her. And of course they could.

I'd never been in a position like that before and it kinda surprised me when I realized that I was now, for the first time. I didn't really know how to handle it except to admit to myself that Manda Reese was worth a hell of a lot more than Howard Blackburn's sheep. If it ever came down to that I supposed I would just have to give in and live with it.

I began to wonder then if this business of caring about somebody else was a very good idea, especially considering the line of work I was in. And I began to wonder just how much I did care for this thin, green-eyed woman who might or might not be a widow and who was coming to mean so much to me so quickly.

I'd known women before, of both the good and the bad variety, and I had enjoyed their company and sometimes more. I enjoyed them while they were handy but never thought a thing before about leaving to go on about my business without them. I'd neither promised nor asked more than that.

Now I wasn't so sure. Now I was starting to wonder where Amanda Reese was going to go from here and if there would be a place for me in the planning. Mostly I wondered if she would want me around longer than both my job and the continued existence of her place might keep us near the other. She had never said either way, and it was not a question I would feel comfortable about asking.

I sighed right out loud and leaned back against the barn wall and toyed with one hammer on my short-barreled scattergun. This was not the sort of problem I was used to handling.

I looked up toward the house. I would have enjoyed being able to see glimpses of her busying around inside or just sitting in her chair with a book laid open in her lap and a pair of knitting needles in her hands—I never could understand how she could read and knit at the same time but she sure did—but of course I could not. The windows were all shuttered and she already had the lights blown out. If she had taken a reading lamp to bed with her she had the light well shielded for I couldn't see anything of the house but a dark-on-dark mass over there.

It was tempting to slip over to the house for a moment but I reached for the coffee gourd instead. I never got it unstoppered. Down below the sheep pen Beggar barked once and began to growl.

A moment later I could hear what he'd detected. Once the dog barked, the raiders quit trying to sneak in and came on hell-for-leather with their pistols working. This wasn't any lone rifleman. This was a whole crowd.

CHAPTER 28

Hoof-pound and pistol shots filled the night air with all the noise it seemed it could carry. Muzzle flashes coming out of that boil of noise showed me they were riding in a compact group and looked to be headed toward the woollies.

I put the coffee bottle down or maybe just left it hanging in the air there; I don't remember which. The shotgun went with me, though, and I went scooting down along the rails between them and my sheep.

They were still a little far for either pistol or shotgun fire to be effective so I hunkered low and waited. It would've been a little safer if I'd stretched out on the ground but I wanted to be able to duck and run as soon as I showed them muzzle blast from my shotgun.

At least by now Manda should know enough to stay where she was with the doors and windows barred and some solid timbers between her and danger.

It took only seconds for them to sweep into range. They were whooping and yelling along with all the other racket they were making. Lordy, some of them must have thought it was some kind of a lark. I put the cold butt of the shotgun to my shoulder and changed that opinion.

I pulled the front trigger and touched off the second right behind it, letting the movement of their own horses shift that load toward a fresh group.

Their yelling had a different quality to it now. Some of them were hurt. Others sounded scared.

I stopped a dozen feet away from where I'd been and jammed a pair of fresh loads into the breech. I turned those loose too although now I was guessing more about where they were. Their firing had really slacked off after my first return shots. I don't believe I hit anything that second time.

They were practically to the pen now, and I palmed my revolver instead of trying to reload again.

I couldn't see much but I could smell the fresh-raised dust and the burned powder as they wheeled their horses back the way they'd come and went tearing off at a dead run. I holstered the revolver and reloaded the shotgun to wait for another charge. It didn't come.

The time dragged as I squatted there against the fence rail with the stubby shotgun raised and ready. I wanted to run for the house and make sure Manda was all right, but I dasn't. She shouldn't be in any danger. The sheep were. I couldn't leave them untended.

I also couldn't understand why they weren't coming again. They had been at long shotgun range the first time I fired so I might've peppered some of them but I shouldn't have hit them real bad. If they had any sand at all they should have gotten themselves back together before now. Popper Morgan had said they were a riding crew and not gunhands, but still . . . any of them along on this jaunt should have known what they were getting into. I didn't understand what they were up to and therefore didn't like it.

The waiting stretched out longer and longer, and eventually I quit trying to stay on edge and let the shotgun relax down into my lap. Still they didn't come.

The evening breeze had been coming down from the north. It eddied as it began to swing from the south. I could smell the dust and the heavy, slightly oily, not at all unpleasant odor of the sheep themselves. As the wind completed its shift there was a new and sharp smell in it that was definitely out of place here. I jumped to my feet and began to run.

That was coal oil I was smelling. Lots of it. If a match hit it . . .

I'd been waiting about midway down the fence on the yard side, and it was too far around to get there before a man could strike a match and drop it. I had no target to shoot at in the darkness. But I could try to get there in time. Whoever was over there might still be dousing the brush or even the sheep themselves with the fuel.

I pounded down to the end of the pen and flung myself around the corner.

The brush I had piled there against the rifle fire took me by surprise. I tripped and went down. I lost my hold on the shotgun. I thought it pitched somewhere into the brush pile but I wasn't sure. And I sure wasn't going to take time looking for it. I bounced back up and ran on, this time remembering to run wider of my brush pile.

I reached the far end of the fence panting air into lungs that felt bathed with fire but I got there in a hurry.

I needn't have bothered.

Beggar was already there. Ahead of me I heard his soft, whining growl that told me he'd done his job but didn't know what to do next. "Where are you, boy?" He kept it up and I felt my way forward.

The coal-oil smell was strong here. Very. It would have been safe enough to strike a match for some light, of course, but I couldn't do that without making a target of myself.

I kept inching forward until I was beside Beggar and my boot toes jabbed into something. I knelt and felt around with my hands. What I'd kicked used to be a man, now it was a body. I found his arm but there was no blood-thump in the wrist. I guess Beggar had done his job, all right.

All the tight-wound tension of the fight drained out of me now and I felt weak and almost limp. I was trembling just a little, which is something I often do after a scrap although never before or during one.

I really wanted now to go up to the house and hold Manda and wait with her for the daylight, but of course I could not. Their little trick hadn't worked, but the LG could come back at any time. They would be waiting somewhere out on the grass right now, not too close but near enough that they could see the expected burst of rising yellow flame when their man touched off the oil. When it didn't come, when they finally decided it wouldn't come, they might try again to rush the place under the cover of the night.

I fondled Beggar's ears and rubbed his head and told him what a fine fellow he was—which I'm sure he already knew but which he always liked to hear anyway—and dried my hands on my britches. The old devil'd had some wet stuff on him that might have been drool but just as likely was somebody's blood. I couldn't tell which it was without a light but I wanted it off my hands.

"Beggar. Guard. Good boy." I went back to the other side of the pen, more slowly this time, and sat at the base of the lower corner post where I could best react no matter which direction they might come from. I tried to find the shotgun too but it was lost until daylight.

The night air felt chilly again but this time I got no clean and invigorating lift from it. Now it only felt coldly unpleasant to me, and I pondered on the difference a mood could make.

I waited a full hour and judged the time by the shift of the stars so I wouldn't cut it short. I gave it a little more for good measure and when they still hadn't come back walked up to the barn for the coffee gourd and tin cup.

The coffee was no longer near hot but the wrapping had at least kept it warm and it was very welcome. I sat and drank it and thought about calling Beggar over for company, but he needed to be down where he was. One man with a match could still do a lot of damage down there. I went back down the fence line to the stout corner post and sat again to wait the night through.

Come the first hint of daylight I got up and stretched cramped muscles and walked around to the other side of the pen.

The man who'd run into Beggar was messy but I was pretty sure he wasn't anybody I'd ever seen before. It was a shame it wasn't Val Hatcher who had tried this particular piece of dirty work, but working with others wasn't his style. Besides, he should be busy showing himself in town for a day or two. They wouldn't want him doing anything that might make people suspicious of him.

There were a pair of oil cans lying on the ground, each of them about a two-gallon size. Both were uncapped and empty. I couldn't tell for sure at this point what all had been splashed with the stuff but it looked like he'd sloshed it on the piled/brush and probably onto some of the sheep also.

I debated what I ought to do with the dead man. The sheriff would probably want the body and a report of it brought in, but there was no way I could leave now. Even if I took Manda with me and the flock, now that the LG had turned to fire as a good idea they might not want to stop just because the woollies didn't happen to be home. When it came down to it I didn't have much choice. I would bury the guy myself as I'd done with poor Brock and let the LG worry about any future explanations.

I went back to the barn for a shovel and began digging the hole a few feet from where he'd fallen.

The soil was rocky and the digging was slow but I was making progress. Until I was interrupted.

The damned dog should have warned me. He was sitting nearby, taking it easy while he watched me work, sitting there with his tongue out and his head tilted at an inquisitive angle. The sight of dead men didn't bother him. He'd seen enough of them before to not be curious now.

Like I said, he should have warned me but I guess he had pretty much accepted the woman as part of the family, and he didn't react to her approach.

"Good morning, Jude, I . . ." She stopped short, a stricken look on her face. The color quickly drained from her features. She kept staring at the thing that was on the ground. Well, it wasn't pretty.

She looked down at the steaming cup of coffee she was carrying and dully said, "I was . . . bringing . . ."

"Sure. Thanks." I climbed out of the hole and took her by the shoulders and led her around the corner so the brush pile would be between her and the dead man. I pushed her down into a sitting position and sat on the ground next to her. "Drink your coffee, Manda. You'll feel better in a minute."

Mechanically she raised the cup to her lips and drank from it. It looked too hot for comfort but she didn't seem to notice.

Beggar seemed to feel her distress too. He lay beside her and put his head in her lap. She began stroking his head with her free hand, and the dog closed his eyes. I swear he looked like he was ready to swoon from all that good attention.

She petted and rubbed him and it was pretty plain she didn't realize it was old Beggar that had done all that damage. At least I don't think she could've been so affectionate with him if she'd known. I wasn't going to tell her and find out.

After a while I brought her back to remembering that this was a victory and not a tragedy by saying, "That fella had already doused the place with coal oil. It's a good thing he didn't get a match lit or we might have lost a good half the sheep and maybe the barn too."

She looked at me. She looked grim but at least she was looking at me. "Yes. It's just . . . so ugly."

"Of course it is," I told her, "and there's no way either of us could feel right about such ugliness if we started it. But we didn't. Remember that, Manda. Anybody that wants to leave us alone can come and go and do as they please and be as safe as church. We haven't started any of it and we won't. Remember that, girl."

She nodded. She seemed to be feeling some better now. "All

right. I'll try." She gave me a weak smile. "This coffee is supposed to be yours, and I've been drinking it. Here."

"We can share it."

"Go on and finish it. I'll have breakfast ready in about ten minutes."

"Give me a shout when it's ready."

She glanced over her shoulder in the general direction of the partially dug grave.

"It's all right. I can leave it whenever you're ready. Go on now."

She sighed and got to her feet. "I won't be long, Jude." Beggar surprised me. He went with her to the house. Me, I got back to digging.

CHAPTER 29

After breakfast I finished burying the raider and did some daylight looking around. Not a one of the wethers had been shot and if any of them had had coal oil poured on them it didn't seem to hurt them any. They all looked and acted normal.

The garden had been trampled some and I found somebody's revolver lying in the yard with two live rounds in it yet. I reloaded it and stashed it in a likely looking spot on the hillside behind and above the house. I thought it would be handy there in case I had to slip out a back window or something.

There weren't any real obvious blood puddles or anything like that to tell me if I'd hit anybody. I still figured if I had it would not have been anything too awfully serious.

I had no more than finished my fooling around at the house and was fixing to take the sheep out to the grass when the sheriff and another rider came into sight. It looked like they hadn't lost any time running to him after their raid failed, judging from the time it would take them to make a round trip to Wolf Creek and back. I went up to the house to be with Manda when they arrived.

"I'll handle the talking if you don't mind," I told her.

"All right, but what do they want?"

I shrugged. "They'll tell us soon enough."

The second man was a stranger to me but Manda made a face like she needed to spit out something foul in her mouth and said, "That's Jay Pyle with him."

"Herring's doing an awful lot of riding these days," I said without any sympathy. I was wishing he had kept things under control better.

Manda allowed them into the house but with a cool reserve that let them know that they wouldn't be treated as guests. I was glad to see, too, that she kept her chin up and her eyes on them. She did not offer them anything to eat or drink either.

Sheriff Herring put his hat on a peg as he'd done before. Pyle took his hat off but held it in his hands instead. I noticed Herring kept his gun on this time.

Pyle was a sandy-haired man of average height or a hair more and his build average or a hair heavier. His mouth was small and, now, tightly held, his eyes close-set and with the attention drawn to them by bags pouched under them. Which was reasonable. He ought to be tired after shooting and riding all night. I suppose I was prejudiced beforehand but I think I would have felt the same if I'd seen him as a passing stranger on the street. What I'm getting at is that just at first sight I didn't like him. Somehow he struck me as being a small man. Not in size, which doesn't mean anything anyway, but small-minded and small-moraled. He seemed of a class with Val Hatcher.

Manda sat prim and poised in her own easy chair and I followed her lead by settling loose and easy in the big armchair I was almost starting to think of as mine.

Manda wasn't going to let any social conventions force her into a politeness she didn't feel or want, either. She came out with it blunt and up front. "I hope you have a good reason for bringing this man onto my property, Arlo."

The two of them had dragged over the hard, straight-backed wooden chairs from the table and were sitting on those, looking a little out of place and uncomfortable. Herring glanced at Pyle before he spoke.

"The, uh, LG asked me to investigate a rather serious matter, Mrs. Reese. They say there was, uh, a shooting incident here. Last night."

The sheriff paused. It was plain he expected Manda to jump into the conversation with some sort of explanation or denial. I was proud of her, though. She didn't wiggle, just sat there with her mouth closed and a patient, almost regal look about her.

"Mr. Pyle," he went on, "said a group from the LG rode over here yesterday evening to try to, uh, negotiate with both of you. He said you, Mr. Priest, opened fire on them without warning. They turned and rode away. When they were out of range they discovered Freeman Luce missing from their party. Rather than get into a gunfight with you they chose to notify me so the law could take its course." Herring sounded like he didn't really accept a quarter of that himself, but it was what had been told to him and now he wanted to get it all straight.

Not that he would baldly accept our side of the story either. Anything we said would be just as suspect as what they told him. He turned to Manda, and of all of us in the room I suspect he trusted her the most. Likely had the most sympathy for her too.

"Mrs. Reese," he asked, "is that story, uh, more or less what happened?"

Manda shook her head firmly. "You know it isn't, Arlo. Jude never would have shot first, and anyway they had no business here. They came after dark and tried to shoot up our sheep. It was their own fault their man was killed."

"And you could testify to that?" Herring asked. "You said it was at night. Did you see what happened?"

She hesitated, and I believe she was wondering if she could get away with a lie. Probably the sheriff's mention of the darkness made the decision for her. And she was right. A good lawyer anxious to please the LG could rip her up on that point. "Not really, Arlo. I was inside the whole time. With my doors and shutters barred. I heard shots. I didn't see any of it."

The sheriff looked pretty well satisfied and I believe he was glad he could figure Manda as being out of this. "What about you, Priest?"

I shrugged. "Somebody came in the night. They started shooting. Rode away when I fired a few rounds back at long range. One of them did manage to get himself killed. I didn't kill him."

Herring's eyebrows went up. Pyle looked smug. Hell, he wouldn't have cared if I was telling the truth. If one of their own bullets had killed their man it would be all right with them. With their word against that of a sheepherder they could pin it on me as murder no matter who'd really shot the guy. I wouldn't be able to prove otherwise to a jury. As far as they knew.

Manda was the only one who seemed really surprised, but then she believed too that it had been my shotgun that tore the dead man's throat out.

"The, uh, other side," Herring said, "tells me they were riding in in plain sight after calling out to you. That you fired as they approached peacefully."

"What kind of gun, sheriff?"

He turned to look at the other man.

Pyle answered it smoothly and what should have been effec-
tively. "He fired twice with a shotgun and several times more with
a pistol. I couldn't say which shot hit Freeman." He smiled thinly.
"Things were pretty confused right then, Arlo. We hadn't expected
to be fired on in cold blood. That Association man, Brock, had
told us we could expect better than that from Judas Priest. Now we
know his name fits him."

Herring turned back to face me. "You'd better ride in to town
with me, son. There won't be any back-door justice. I can promise
you that. But I imagine the hearing will mean at least a man-
slaughter charge, maybe murder. You can call in any lawyer you
want, and I can promise you you'll still be alive for the trial date."

"I believe you, sheriff. But I don't think you'll want to take me in
after you've seen the evidence."

I was talking to Herring but I was looking at Pyle and grinning
into his face. He was ready, all right. He had his hand hooked and
ready, poised over his gunbelt. If I tried to jump he'd've had his revolver out and working before I could take two steps. Of course
that could work two ways, but he'd feel safe enough with two-to-
one odds.

Even if I'd wanted or needed to handle it that way, though, I
wouldn't have started anything with Manda right there. As it was I
didn't figure I needed to worry. Other places, with other sheriffs, I
might have. I didn't believe I needed to here. I hoped I was right.

"Before you go making a charge, sheriff, let's take a look at Pyle's
dead friend. You'll want to take him in anyway."

Herring nodded. "All right. Meantime I'd like you to take that
gun off. I'd kinda feel better if you did."

"I don't think so, sheriff. You haven't charged me with anything
yet. And your friend there . . . let's just say I don't wanta be walking any lighter than him, huh?"

"Jay. Hang your gun over there. Priest can do the same. No
charges. Just so everybody can get along comfortably. All right?"

Pyle didn't like it. He scowled and dragged his heels and made it
plain he did not like doing this. "Go on, Jay," Herring prodded,
and the man did. The sheriff turned back to me.

I nodded and unbuckled my belt. When I stood I let it stay there
in the chair. I didn't exactly like the feeling either. In a way I could
sympathize with Jay Pyle. When I walked it felt oddly uncom-

fortable without that weight where it belonged. It felt like some part of me was missing.

"Where is he?" Herring asked.

"The other side of the sheep pen. I buried him this morning."

Again the sheriff's eyebrows went up.

I shrugged. "I didn't know how the LG's would want to handle this. After a while bodies start to smell. He shouldn't be bad yet." I paused and turned to Manda. "You might want to stay here."

"I'd like to know what's happening, Jude."

"Please. It's all right. Really."

Reluctantly she nodded, and I led the way down toward the pens.

I stopped at the gate to let the sheep out and put Beggar to taking them down onto the grass. It was long past time they got some graze, and I couldn't see any point in having the dog there when Pyle found out he'd been the one to take their man down.

The delay, especially for a bunch of sheep, really graveled Pyle. But then I wasn't much concerned about what he wanted. Herring didn't seem to mind. I took my time about it and got Beggar well started with the flock before I took them on around to where I'd buried Pyle's man.

"Right there, sheriff," I said, pointing to the freshly turned earth. "I'll provide the shovel. Pyle can dig up his own sheep butcher." I got a shovel from the barn—both of them trailing with me to watch what I was doing—leaned it against the pen rails and folded my arms. I'd dug that ground once. They could do the rest.

A half hour later Herring's grim looks were directed at Pyle and not me. "Take your man and get out of here, Jay. And his oil cans. If Priest wants to file some sort of charge against you—and Lord knows he and Mrs. Reese have enough they could pick from—you'd better be available to answer them."

The man meant it, too. You could hear it in his voice. He sounded so straight I almost told him about Brock, but I didn't. That might have been too much.

"I'll think it over, sheriff. We have to be in town Thursday for that other hearing anyway. I'll let you know then." If I sounded like I was trying to hold back a chuckle it's because I was. "For now I hope you won't mind if I tell this . . . *person* to get the hell off the 2R. I don't think Mrs. Reese wants him here any more than I do."

Herring nodded. "We'll leave. Right now."

"You aren't being counted in with him, sheriff."

He pulled at his chin, "Yeah, well . . . I'd better go along with the body anyway. We'll want the county coroner to take a look. Make everything proper and official, just in case."

"I hadn't thought of that," I told him, which was the truth. "I'll bring his gun down from the house now if you want to get the body loaded." I guess I didn't have to add that I'd feel a lot better when I had my own gun where it belonged. "And sheriff. Thanks." I gave Pyle my very best, most insolent grin and turned away.

CHAPTER 30

"What will they do now, Jude?" She had come down to the barn after they left, as if seeking reassurance. Or maybe just company.

"I wish I could tell you. Whatever it is I don't believe they'll quit. If anything they'll be more anxious than before to get it settled before we go in for that court thing Thursday. They won't want us filing any charges against them. That sheriff of yours just might be fool enough—or honest enough—to go an' enforce the law. They wouldn't like that."

She shivered. "This is Tuesday. And we have to leave for town tomorrow."

"Uh huh. That doesn't give them much time, does it?"

"I don't like this, Jude."

"No sensible person could, girl." I took up the heavy rifle and slipped my free arm around her waist. "Walk with me down to check on the sheep. Clean air and a clear sky'll put things back in proper order, Manda. Whatever the LG does, they can't touch those. Or the grass. Remember that, okay?"

She nodded but she seemed to be far from convinced. Well, so was I really. What I was trying to do was comfort her a little, and I think maybe it was doing a bit of good anyway. Not much but a little.

We walked down the shallow, barely noticeable slope to where the sheep were spread out grazing. Beggar came trotting over with his tongue out and his tail, what there was of it, in happy motion. He took up a position near Manda and walked with us.

"Maybe you're right, Jude." She stopped and turned her face up to the morning sun. A hint of breeze picked up the ends of her hair and played with them. "It really is a pretty day, isn't it."

"And a pretty woman," I added.

Her green eyes came back down to earth and locked onto mine. She looked at me for what seemed a long time before she spoke. "I know better than that, Jude. I'm too thin and much too plain and I look older than I am. You don't have to be gallant, you know."

"I meant it, Manda." And I had. I hoped she could hear the truth of it, and I believe that she did.

Her expression softened and she moved in closer against me. She pushed her face into my shoulder and stood wordlessly for a moment. When she raised her eyes to me again she whispered, "I wish . . . things could've been simpler."

"Don't ask for more than you have, Manda. Especially when what you have is good."

She smiled. "It *is* good, isn't it, Jude. I'm glad for that. Really glad."

I felt a stirring within me that was more than simple wanting. I wanted to hold this woman and protect her and keep her safe. And the act of putting an arm around her was not enough. I wanted to hold her closer than that, more than my arms or any other physical thing could accomplish. I didn't really know what I wanted to do and for lack of knowing I pulled her head tight to me and felt the warmth of her breath in the hollow of my shoulder. That seemed to ease my need, at least temporarily.

After a time she disengaged herself from me and gave me a smile that I thought particularly brave and lovely. She moved forward and came up on her toetips to kiss me lightly. "Get on with your work, Jude, and I'll do mine. I'll call you for lunch."

"All right." I watched her walk back toward the house. I liked to watch her in motion. Long, purposeful, flowing strides. She didn't walk like a man—anything but—but she didn't mince around with dainty little hip-swinging prances either. She was too much woman to have to make a big thing of it, to herself or to anybody else.

Beggar had the sheep well in hand. Hell, half the time I felt bad about taking pay for herding sheep. He did nearly all the real work. But then, there were times when I was needed too.

I sat on the ground among the sheep—there was no point in making a standing target of myself—and listened to the faint sounds of the busily eating wethers. For some reason they are quieter about their grazing than either a cow or a horse. Now that they were on the grass and content they weren't even blatting their usual protests.

I sat feeling the sun on my back, lazily watching the horizon some but mostly keeping an eye on Beggar to alert me if anyone came around. Toward noon Manda came out and clanged a dinner call on her iron. I chirped to Beggar and had him help me move the sheep up to the pen. I didn't want them left alone even that short length of time so I pulled them in while we ate.

Later, relaxed and comfortably full from a huge omelet, I let myself get lazy. I let Beggar take the flock out of the pen again and wandered back up to the house for another cup of Manda's good coffee.

She gave me the refilled cup and a brief peck on the lips even though she'd already been up to her elbows in dishwater when I came back in, then she turned me around in the direction of the big easy chair. I was feeling about as content and mellow as a man could.

I bent to slouch down into that comfortable chair but I never got there. I hadn't much more than started down when I heard the shot.

I have no idea what became of that full cup of steaming hot coffee. Whether I dropped it, threw it aside or even set it down I just wouldn't know. Before I had time to think about it I was at the door with the heavy high-sidewall in my hand and a stab of fear wrenching my gut. Manda was safely inside. So was I. But there was still a friend of mine out there, a friend who the night before had killed one of the LG raiders.

That was the first thought that hit me when I heard the familiar sound of the rifleman's weapon. Beggar was out there with no protection.

Anxious as I was, though, I wasn't fool enough to go running out into the yard where the rifleman could take a crack at me too.

"Get the shutters," I said. "No. Wait. I'll do that." It sounded like he was shooting from the hillside, probably somewhere down past the barn, but I wasn't going to risk having him shoot at Manda if I was wrong. And even if I was right he might've moved since that first round. "Bring a chair over here against the wall, Manda. Wait right there in it until I tell you different."

I slipped from window to window pulling the shutters to and dropping their heavy bars into place. From each fresh angle I tried to spot Beggar. I could see the sheep all right. They were out on the grass not a half mile off, bunched and grazing quietly.

But I couldn't see Beggar from any of the house windows. He was down. For sure he was down. If he hadn't been he would be on guard now between the flock and the danger or else racing up here to get back to me.

There was a deep, intense coldness inside me. It lay hard and tight in my belly as I closed the last shutter without being able to see the old dog. There still had been no second shot. This time Hatcher had no intention of pinpointing himself with round after round thrown at the relatively worthless sheep. This time he was serious about his work. And a man who could hit a large dog at probably seven or eight hundred yards . . . that was very serious indeed.

Manda was where I'd told her to be. She sat with her hands un-fumbling at her knitting and her green eyes following me with interest but with no apparent fear.

I checked my pockets. I had a full box of twenty cartridges in my left-hand coat pocket, four loose rounds from a previous boxful in a trouser pocket and one round in the chamber. That was plenty. More than plenty. The one in my rifle might be enough. If I got to use it.

"Manda. I want you to bar the door behind me. I don't know how long I'll be gone. When I come back I won't knock. I'll tell you who I am and what I want. If you hear a knock, even groaning or carrying on like I'm in awful pain, it ain't me. Don't open the door to anybody else. You understand me?"

"Yes." Her eyes were solemn, her face composed. She opened her mouth to speak again but remembered in time and shut it again. It was plain she had willed herself against questions or protest. "I'll do just what you say, Jude. Please be . . ."

I grinned at her. "I'll be careful, Manda."

I headed for the door and again she visibly forced back a protest.

"He's up on the hill," I told her. "He'll expect me to try an' slip out the back. So I'll use the door." At least I hoped that was what he would be expecting.

"Come on now. Bar this door as soon as I'm out. I can't be worrying about you while I'm out there." She hurried to my side. There was no point in waiting longer. I took up my rifle and stepped out into the open.

CHAPTER 31

There was no cover here at the front of the house. I felt naked and vulnerable. I've faced men with guns before. A good many times before. I've been shot at from ambush by men with rifles. But this was the first time I had locked horns with an expert at long-range precision shooting. This was something else entirely.

The fear was not new, of course. Anyone with half a grain of sense should be afraid when someone with a gun comes to kill him. There is the fear that burns inside, the terrible awareness of how thin a covering cloth and skin really are. The thing, though, is to not dwell on it, to not wait and think and stay afraid but to go ahead with doing whatever can be done.

I didn't stand on the front stoop thinking about this now, and I didn't go bolting for the cover of the barn as I figured he might expect me to do. If he was waiting out on the grass I couldn't stand there at the front of the house and make his shot easy for him. If he was behind on the hill—where I figured him to be—he'd likely expect to see me on the right of the house between it and the barn. So I ducked off to the left and ran around toward the walled-up spring, moving low and fast and with my attention on the hillside.

It was tempting to drop behind the solid-rock protection of the spring wall, but that would have been a mistake. One of the things I had going for me—one of the few things since Val Hatcher was a craftsman who had had plenty of time to pick his waiting place—was speed. I needed to move fast enough that he wouldn't have time to recover from the surprise and line up a running shot. If I stopped before I was into heavier cover he would be waiting for me the next time.

One thing about a marksman is that he is almost never a snap shooter. It takes a while to find and line up a tube or vernier sight. And a twenty-pound barrel is slow to swing. Give him time and a rifleman like Hatcher could damn near shave you, one whisker at a time. But if his target is there for only a glimpse and then is gone, he probably won't waste a shot trying for something he hasn't got good aim at.

Of course that works both ways. I had a far-reaching rifle myself so this wasn't going to turn into some rapid-fire scrap in the woods. The next shot either of us fired could be the one to decide the whole thing.

And the next shot likely would be his.

That was probably the worst of it. He would probably have to shoot again before I would have any idea where he was.

So far the only place I knew the man *wasn't* was inside the house with Manda. He could be absolutely anywhere else within a half mile or so of the house. Anywhere.

Normally that wouldn't have been any big problem. I could cluck to Beggar and the old dog would get to work on it and let me know where he was. Now . . . I guess I hadn't ever paid much attention to how much that mongrel dog did for me.

And I had to know where Hatcher was waiting. I like to think that I'm pretty good at using cover, any kind that's available, but no one is good enough to keep himself hidden from all sides at once. Not short of crawling into a hole and waiting for someone to come finish you off, that is. So if I guessed wrong I could move right into Hatcher's line of fire.

Oh, I would do my guessing. I'd have to. But unless I had the impossibly wild, dumb luck to catch sight of a carefully hidden man I wouldn't really know where he was until he opened up with that big rifle again. And if he was half as good as he was supposed to be, or used to be, I was going to need a good deal of luck to make it past that shot.

I could think and plan and hope and try, but mostly I could keep moving.

I charged past the spring and scrambled up onto the hillside.

There was brush here at least. From the garden and down on the grass below it I would still be exposed. To both sides and to a lesser extent from above, though, I had some protection. I didn't have to be behind a solid barrier, of course, like Manda was inside the log house. If he couldn't see me he couldn't shoot me because now, while I didn't know where he was, was no time for the kind of haphazard searching fire he'd used during those long nights of the past week.

I bellied down into the mat of old needles and leaves and tried to regain control of my breathing. It hadn't been that much of a run from the house to the hillside, but the placement of a rifle bullet is kinda sensitive to heaving breath or a jumpy heartbeat. This was no time to be forgetting things like that.

The deep, penetrating smell of decaying leaves and the lighter, drier smell of long-dead needles were close and cool in my nostrils. Other times I could've settled back and really enjoyed them. Even now I was strongly enough aware of them to like and appreciate them. But lying there with my nose buried in the ground wasn't getting Val Hatcher located.

I shifted my rifle into both hands, ready to raise and fire as soon as I had a target. It was an awkward and heavy thing, but it was accurate. If it had been fast to fire too it would've been ideal.

It took only a few minutes for the birds and whatever other small creatures there were on this hillside to get over their fright at my disturbance. They began making their low and brief but all too frequent noises. Chirps and chittering, rustle of leaves and the soft rasp of claws on bark or wingtips dragging through brush. Few of their noises were loud but there were many of them.

Their racket, little as it was, made my job all the harder. A hunt in brush is conducted far more by sound than by sight, for sound travels through the screening cover of foliage that will hide game. Or a man. Any disturbance is sure to catch the attention of those who bother to listen closely, even as little as the sound of cloth being drawn against rock. The normal sounds of a peaceful hillside just would help to hide any faint noise Hatcher might make.

And he didn't need his ears to know where I was. Wherever he was he was sure to have seen my run from the house to hiding. Right now he should know within ten feet where I was.

Worse, he didn't have to do any moving around and noisemaking. He could stay right where he was and wait for me to come after him. If I didn't he could just wait for dark and pull out, able to choose the time and place for another try. If I wanted him it was up to me to go get him.

And oh, how I did want him. In the back of my brain, burning there ever since I heard that first shot, was the cold, empty, ugly knowledge that he'd shot a friend of mine, the only close and constant friend I'd had in many years. For that I wanted Val Hatcher, and I wanted him now.

It was still early enough that it should be over before I'd need to worry about running out of daylight so I took my time and waited until my breathing was slowed to normal before I moved again.

I wasn't interested in preserving my dignity now. I went up that hillside on my belly, worming from cover to cover, trying to use every tiny fold in the ground to keep from exposing myself to him.

After fifty yards or so I stopped and slipped into a steep-backed hollow or maybe an ancient washout where I could see out onto the grass below without exposing myself to either side. It was time to do some looking and some thinking.

I believed Hatcher was somewhere on that hillside overlooking the ranch, but I wasn't willing to bet my life on it.

From here I could see over the house to the grazing sheep. I couldn't see Beggar down there, though, and I figured he'd been dropped flat into the grass and so might be hidden from me.

It wasn't a dead dog I was looking for anyway. I wanted the rifleman who had shot him, and I began an inch-by-inch search of the grass from a half mile and inward.

Most people don't know it—never need to learn it—but a grown man can hide himself on bare, grassless dirt simply by lying flat and staying still. Unless a searcher really knows what he is looking for his eyes will sweep right over a still object.

Especially when there is a lot of open ground to be searched a man will swing his eyes across a broad field of view. Movement will catch his eye doing that but never a stationary target, not even someone wearing bright colors as a rule. A man in drab clothes is almost always safe if he doesn't move.

The trick to finding an ambusher on open ground is to not let your eyes sweep in those long, temptingly easy arcs. It takes patience and a lot of firm reminders to yourself but if you really want to search an area like that what you do is look at one little area at a time. I mean really look it over. Then move on to another small section and really stare at it. It's the only way to be sure of seeing everything in view.

I took my time about it and inspected one patch at a time. There is a tendency too to overlook the obvious so I took particular care about looking over the garden and the pens and the area in and near the ranch yard itself. It took a while but eventually I was satisfied that Hatcher wasn't out on the grass or anywhere in the 2R headquarters that I could see. It was what I'd expected but now I wasn't gambling on that.

The next question was where to go from here. Both the rule and the instinct of the hunt are to get higher, to get above whatever you are after whether it is a mule or a man. Soldiers tell me it's the same in the Army. If you hold the high ground you have the advantage.

But Hatcher would know that as well as I did. He'd be expecting me to climb. He knew I was on the hill. By now he shouldn't know exactly where any longer but he would know I was somewhere on that hill. He would expect me to try to get above him.

Or he might be expecting me to try to outsmart him by moving along the hillside instead of up it. He could already be trying to outclimb me or he could be holed up somewhere with his muzzle trained downhill waiting for me to crawl right under it. Rather than get myself into a confusing circle of trying to go one step farther than him in a game of who's gonna outwit who I suppose I just as easily could've flipped a coin to decide which I should try.

In the end I decided not to fret over it. The rule about climbing is a good many times older than I'll ever be, and rules like that are accepted as rules for just one reason: They work. I took a fresh grip on my rifle and began climbing again.

Higher up, the hillside was choppy and rugged, covered with dark evergreens and with a lot of naked rock showing through the thin soil. There was no timberline here to try to get above—the Black Hills weren't high enough for that, I guess—but up higher the trees did thin out quite a bit and there was a whole lot of hill up there to be climbed.

I crawled higher, slow and careful for the better part of an hour. At the end of that time I hadn't accomplished a thing except get a little higher and get myself good and dirty. I stopped again and began searching the hill for Val Hatcher.

If it isn't easy to see a man hiding on open ground it's even harder to see one hiding under cover. What most people seem to do is look for a man. A whole one. Or a deer or whatever. You just can't do that.

If you look for a person you'll see nothing but trees. What you look for is a piece of what you're after. An eye or a boot, a hatbrim or an ear or something like that. But never the whole thing.

I took my time again and began looking, not for Val Hatcher but for some small part of him or his gear.

What I found was just what had grown, fallen or been dragged onto that part of Manda Reese's hillside. But no Val Hatcher.

From here I had a broader view of the grass rolling out like a great inland lake to the next hill east, and so I looked that over again—more quickly this time—and the ranch buildings and surrounding area. The house from here was nothing but a roof. Manda was in there—safe, I hoped—no matter what else happened.

I rolled over onto my belly and began climbing again. It was then that Val Hatcher fired his second shot of the fight.

CHAPTER 32

The bullet came ripping across the front of my body, flying in unexpected and out of nowhere it seemed, and I was so startled I jumped backward and went tumbling and skittering down the slope for a dozen feet before I piled up against the bole of a tree.

It hadn't been a bad shot and if I'd been a little fatter and heavier through the body it would have sliced me open like a saber slash. As it was the slug passed under my arm and across my belly, tearing some cloth and raising a bright-red weal on my forearm that hurt like the very devil even if it wasn't a serious wound. It seeped and oozed a little but wasn't really bleeding.

A quick glance told me that much and then I was scrambling back up toward a protecting hump in the ground.

Hatcher was off to my left not fifty yards away. Probably I'd surprised and scared him just as much as he had me, showing up unexpected on a level with him and so close. He would've been expecting to see me and get a careful shot while I was still well below him and not knowing where he was. He obviously hadn't been aware of the cover I'd been able to use to get so near him.

It was both the surprise and the fact that I was so close that led to my still being alive now. When I'd stopped to take that long look around he'd been that close by the whole time and neither of us aware of the other. When I went to climb again he had seen me and had taken a snap shot at me.

With a regular saddle carbine or a shotgun he likely would have had me cooling by now, but a far-reaching rifle is not made for this kind of close, rapid work and he'd been just a hair off.

By now he would be reloaded, and both of us were ready. Scared and falling or no, I sure hadn't turned loose of my rifle when I went tumbling, and now I was ready.

I wriggled across the slope on my belly to the base of another tree and peeped around it. I was hugging the ground so close it's a wonder I wasn't plowing a furrow with my nose.

I had no trouble finding his position. Behind one of those slight, irregular humps in the steep, rocky soil I could see a faint flutter that was his hair riffling in the breeze and nearby I made out the top of what looked like a globe-front sight. There wasn't any of his head showing for me to shoot at and after a moment the bit of hair disappeared as well.

Probably he would lie there and wait a while on the chance that I was dead or dying.

I thought back to the moment of his shot and tried to remember my body motions at the time. I had been scared and had bucked away from the feel of the bullet's passage. There had been no sound of lead hitting meat, but at such a near range you often won't hear that. It comes too close after the sound of the rifle shot itself to be heard separately.

I tried to imagine how my reaction would've looked from where he was and decided he might well think he had hit me a solid one. If I was lucky he would wait a while and then come look at the body. If he tried to come in I would have him.

My rifle was just as poor for this short-range stuff as his was. Wonderfully accurate at a distance but terrible slow for close work.

The vernier sight mounted on its spindly-looking riser back at the end of the tang was what made it so slow. Accurate but slow. I debated on it and decided to fold the thing down out of the way in its carrying position. That left me with no rear sight but I figured at this distance I could shoot with a bare barrel a lot faster and not too awful bad in the accuracy department. I pushed the arm down and lowered it carefully so it didn't slap metal against metal. I thought about letting out an artistic groan but decided that might be more warning than invitation. If he was thinking me already dead he was welcome to keep it up.

I waited but so did Val Hatcher. He would likely give me a half hour to do my dying in, I figured, so I decided to give him forty-five minutes. If he didn't come in that amount of time I'd try to work my way above and around him.

It was a combination of simple impatience and plain dumb luck— and maybe a touch of caution too to be honest about it—that made me do some generalized rubber-necking in a direction other than the one where I'd seen Hatcher.

He was down below me. I caught a flash of movement down there. He hadn't waited long and he hadn't been sure enough or bold enough to walk right over, either. Nor had he tried to climb for his look-see at the body. This was one canny fellow and no one to take lightly.

I saw that hint of motion and then another. My rifle was cocked and ready without my even thinking about it. The next glimpse of him I had I didn't try to aim. I just let my eye and trigger finger take over and do their work. I drove a shot downhill at the patch of light brown that was his jacket or a part of it.

There isn't much smoke that comes out of a rifle barrel, especially a long one, but there was enough to cloud my view of what was down there at that instant after firing. By the time I could see clearly again, Hatcher was no longer in sight. Right then I was really wishing I had carried the shotgun instead of the rifle.

I wasn't going to wait for him to get himself collected now. I rolled sharply right and scrambled above the protection of a fallen, decaying log. Only then did I take time to reload the long rifle.

Now it was my turn to wonder if I'd hit him and, if I had, how hard. Well, I wasn't going to be any dumber than him about walking down to see. If he took me he was going to have to earn it. I wasn't going to throw myself into his lap as a reward for him being such a nice fella.

If he was still alive—and I had to figure that he was—he would be waiting for me to come down looking for him. But I could take a lesson from his book. Instead of going straight down toward where I'd seen him last I began crawling slowly across toward where he had been when he shot at me.

There was a fair amount of cover and I made it to the spot without drawing any more fire.

Once there my curiosity made me turn and look across from his ambush to the place where I'd been when he fired. The man was an awfully good shot. From this angle he had practically no target over there to shoot at but he'd made the absolute most of it. I rubbed the sticky, painful bullet burn on my forearm and let out a breath that I hadn't realized I was holding.

I took a quick look around on the ground too, but as I'd expected there was no sign of him being here except for some crushed leaves that might or might not have been caused by him. There were no cigarette butts or pipe dottle, certainly no empty cartridge cases left and forgotten. I followed the covering-ground contour down from there, almost certainly following the same route he would've taken when he left his ambush.

Another bullet clipped twigs over my head and sent a fall of short needles down onto my hat. I rolled right and slid downhill in a fast, noisy hurry. He was above me again, about where I'd been earlier.

He was shooting almost wildly now and I guess I was too. I drove a shot back toward him without really expecting to hit anything. I'd have given my next year's pay, or several, to have my shotgun in my hands now. I jumped to my feet and ran for a dense clump of young growth twenty-five or thirty yards farther along the hillside.

A bullet from Hatcher's rifle reached the trees about the same time I did but not close enough to worry about. I ducked in among them and threw myself down to reload. I started crawling uphill again.

Val Hatcher was shooting wildly now, at least for him. Every five to ten seconds he would send another round smashing into the young, low-growing cedars or whatever these feathery things were. He was always fairly close and undoubtedly he could hear me moving steadily up the hill. There was enough of an outward curve in the ground between us, though, that his bullets couldn't get down in the dirt to where I was hugging the ground and driving upward with my legs.

He was holed up about seventy-five or eighty yards away, behind the same log where I'd lain myself a little while before. For some reason he seemed to have decided to make a stand there.

I kept climbing, trying to ignore his bullets and the thought that the shape of this hillside was not constant. A lucky bullet—or an unlucky one—could find me at any time.

I reached a protecting knoll or knob on the hillside, most of it bare rock, and crawled around to the far side of it. As soon as I knew it was safe I came onto my feet and sprinted back along the hillside to a point directly above him. Cautiously then, not even giving myself time for my breathing to settle, I began lowering myself down the steep slope toward him. Or toward where I *thought* he was. He might have moved too while I was behind that knob.

CHAPTER 33

He wasn't firing now, but in a way I wished he would. At least then I would know for sure where he was. But then he couldn't be positive about where I was either. Climbing up here I'd been interested in speed more than stealth. Now it was just the other way around. Now a noise could kill me.

Now every fallen twig or unsoggy leaf was an enemy for I no longer had the protection of solid earth between me and Val Hatcher's big rifle, and there was a whole lot less brushy cover than I might have asked for too.

The hillside was steep here so that every foot of the way was a struggle to stay quiet and keep my hold on my rifle and not go falling down, all of them at the same time.

I took my time about it. I had to. I resented every tick of that time, though, for it was that much longer since I'd been sure of Hatcher's position. If he had moved—and he might very well have done it—he could be damn near anywhere on the slope by now.

It was an out-and-out game of cat and mouse, and I didn't know which I was.

The log where Hatcher had been hiding was in plain sight now. I couldn't see a thing there except age-peeled and gray old wood. I had to keep on assuming that Hatcher hadn't moved, but I didn't have to be in a rush about it. I stopped where I was and took a careful look to both sides.

The air felt kinda chill now and I finally realized why. The sun was long since gone behind the hill and it was starting to come evening. If I didn't hurry we might be groping around after each other in the dark. Or, worse, he might pull out and wait to pick himself a better time.

I had a chance to finish it now, though, and if I did there would be no crooked witness to testify against Manda. Lawrence Greenough could hire gun-heavy yahoos by the bucketful and send them after me and Howard Blackburn's sheep for as long as the man's money held out. But the man would play hell trying to convince people that he had a second surprise witness to that cattle deal. If I could take Hatcher now *that* at least should be done for good.

So all right, I decided. Nobody gets to live forever. I hauled back the hammer of my rifle and checked to make sure my revolver was where it ought to be and came up running.

The hillside hadn't gotten any gentler just because I was trying to run down it. I lost my footing and went sliding down on my rump, and if Hatcher hadn't heard me by now he was already dead.

He came up over that log with his head and shoulders clear and that big gun in his hands. Lordy but it did look big.

I was close enough to see his face. He was calm and intent. He'd lost his hat somewhere if he had been wearing one, and his hair was disheveled. If there was any nervousness in him, though, it didn't show in the eyes peering at me across the length of the rifle barrel.

I was sliding and bumping and bouncing around way too much to even try to use my rifle, and he knew it. He was just waiting as I slithered down to him. He seemed to look almost amused.

A sharp outcrop of rock dug into my back and shoulder and came near to bouncing me onto my side. I lost my hold on my rifle with my left hand and went to waving it around in the air. When it seemed to be pointing generally downhill I went ahead and yanked the trigger.

The shot split the air and nothing else, and I doubt the bullet came anywhere within twenty feet of Val Hatcher. I was still slipping and sliding down the hill.

Hatcher was facing an empty rifle now. He sat the rest of the way up and drew down on me with his big gun.

I was close enough now, though. I dug my heels into the soil and kicked myself upright with my left hand out to grab some brush and help to steady me. My belly gun was out and talking.

Hatcher's gun finally fired, but not at me. He'd taken a bullet somewhere in the body.

Hatcher flipped over backward and out of sight. I ended up half hanging from and half standing near the scrub I'd grabbed hold of. My rifle was somewhere behind me and Hatcher's was still in plain sight lying against my side of the log.

I was breathing considerable heavy and my heart was pumping so that I could hear it in my ears. It would be fair to say that I was scared, and I had a case of the nervous shakes for the first time in years.

My knees felt kinda weak and I let myself drop back down into a sitting position. I sat there for a time with my head down but with my eyes open and my gun in my hand.

I couldn't wait long. It would soon be dark. After a few minutes I looked up and called, "Val?"

He said something or made some sort of noise but it was too low for me to make out what it was.

"You have a belly gun, Val. Throw it out where I can see it."

A minute later—it seemed a long time anyway—it came flying over the log. That was the one I knew about. There could be another.

I felt almost too tired to care. Not quite, really. To say that would be a lie. But almost. I wondered if I was getting too old for this business I was in.

I got up and walked downhill, heading for the low end of the old log angled across the slope. When I got close enough that he should've heard which end of the log I was headed for I changed direction and catfooted it toward the upper end of the log.

The precaution hadn't been necessary. Val Hatcher was on the ground there with his hands empty. Or at least with no gun in them. He had other things on his mind right then and had his hands up against his belly hugging himself like that contact was all that was holding him together. He didn't even see me there.

I went in between him and the log and sat down on the log about at his knee level so he could see me without having to raise his head. It took a moment but eventually his eyes moved over toward me and some recognition came into them. There was something else there too, a hard, cold, deep pain that went beyond anything I'd yet known. It was almost like a blanket that limited the depth of any other feeling that might ever be shown there again.

He seemed to be studying on me for a long while. When he finally did open his mouth to speak his gums and the inside of his lips were stained with a thin and watery but very bright red. He had to be busted up pretty bad in there, bad enough that he had to know it.

"Not like this," he said. "I never thought it would be like this." His voice was stronger and clearer than I would have expected.

"To be shot yourself after doing for so many?" I asked, and his eyebrows lifted. "Oh, I know about you, Hatcher. I used to anyway. You used to be kinda famous down in South Texas. That's been a while ago."

Red froth bubbled on his lips when he grinned. "I still am. Should I have heard about you?"

"You would have if you'd lived farther west." That seemed somehow to satisfy him, as if it made a difference whether he was killed by someone else who'd earned that kind of reputation or by some farmer with a pitchfork in his hands. As for myself I couldn't see there would be a difference, but then I wasn't the one doing the dying.

"No," he said, and at first I couldn't remember what he was answering. He went on, "It's always possible. Always the chance someone else would get lucky. When I thought about it, though, I always thought if it happened I'd go clean and quick. A belly wound. That's bad."

"You don't seem to be feeling it that bad."

"Not yet. Shock. I've seen it before. Lots of times. It gets bad later. Must be awful. I never yet saw a man who could take it. They all scream. Beg for it to end. I've seen it before."

"I'll just bet you have, Val."

Again his eyebrows came up.

"What's so surprising, Val? What did you expect? Sympathy? Regrets?" I shook my head. "Hell no, man. I'm the one that shot you, remember? Better you than me, mister."

He gave me another of those bloody grins. "You're a hard man, Priest. Or whatever your name is. Would I know it?"

"You might." I told him what it used to be.

He managed to get out a chuckle. "Well I'll be damned. I've worked for your daddy a couple times."

"Then I'm doubly glad I shot you. How is the old man anyhow?"

"Just like me. Dead. I hated to see him go. He always paid on the spot. Good ol' boy, your father."

"He was shot?"

"No, nothing exciting. Had a storm on a bad horse and broke his neck. A year ago, maybe more."

I nodded and tried to take that in, but I knew the whole of it would have to wait until later to be pondered and accepted. The news did touch me. Even after all this time I had to admit that. But there was also a feeling there that was kind of a lightness, like a burden had been taken from me. That may be a bad thing, even an awful thing to feel from such news, but there it was. Later I could try to take it apart and understand it. For now it was enough that I was aware of it.

"That's all? No weeping and wailing? Well, I said you're a hard man."

I shrugged. "Everybody dies, Hatcher, and that old man was about as sorry as you. Maybe eventually we'll run out of your kind."

"Don't count on it. Not so long as there's men who will put their money down."

"There seems to be aplenty of those. Have you worked for Greenough before?"

"I can't see why I should tell you."

I grinned at him. "Of course you don't have to. I can just walk away any time I want. Leave you here to scream your way out alone. Or better yet I can sit and listen to the great Val Hatcher beg."

He blanched white, and I don't think it had anything to do with pain. Not physical pain anyway. He was a proud man, prideful in some strange and twisted way of who he was and what he did. It would gravel him to think that I might make a barroom story of how Val Hatcher died crying and begging. The truth was that I couldn't see any reason why I'd even want to think about the man again, much less talk about him. But he wouldn't know that.

"You wouldn't do that, would you?"

"I can't see why not. I caused it. I guess I can see it through to the end."

"Look . . . you could finish it for me. Or give me a gun so I can do it."

"You threw a perfectly good one away not fifteen minutes ago. You must not really want one."

"I fell on it. The first time you hit me. Something's broken or I would have used it."

The first time? I took a closer look then and finally saw that his left boot was torn and bloody too. It must have been early in the fight. That explained why he was holed up here and hadn't tried to slip away. He hadn't been able to.

"You know, Val, this is turning out to be just one hell of a hard-luck day for you. I feel for you, man. I really do."

He wound up and did some cussing then. He'd pretty much spoken like a regular gentleman before but whatever his background was it hadn't kept him from learning some potent cusswords and a right good assortment of really colorful descriptive suggestions that he spoke in Spanish. When he unwound I nodded and smiled my appreciation of the way he'd strung it all together.

"Not bad, Val. I haven't heard some of those Mex words since I left Texas."

He started to add to them but all of a sudden stiffened. His face drained of the last bit of color and sweat began pouring off of him. "Oh, God," he moaned.

"He ain't listening to you, Val. The shock's wearing off, huh?"

The look he gave me then was pure agony. "Help me, damn you. Help me."

"I can't see any reason why I should."

"Greenough. You asked about him. Is that what you want? I worked for him before. Once. Last year." He sounded downright eager to please. And I guess now there was only one thing he might possibly have left to hold valuable. That was his pride, and he would lose it if I chose to take it away from him.

"Tell me about it."

"It was Reese, of course. One shot. Good and clean." He did sound proud. It was almost as if he was getting onto me now for not killing him clean.

"On the trail?"

"Uh huh. Nebraska. Near Forty-mile Station. He had . . ." He had to stop for a minute. The pain drew his mouth out of shape, exposing his teeth in an ugly mockery of a grin. "He had the herd spotted for me. Met me at the station. Took me out there. I made the shot easy. Helped drive them in to the station. Sold them for cash to a buyer named Ramey. Out of Chicago. He thought Greenough was Reese. Greenough paid me out of that money. Bonus too. Four hundred for the job and a fifty-dollar bonus on top."

"It was Greenough himself?"

"Uh huh. He wouldn't . . . wouldn't trust Pyle. Me neither. That sonuvabitch would turn on anybody for the right price."

"Where'd you bury Reese?"

The pain was coming harder and faster now. He gave me directions between seizures that racked and weakened him.

With that body and some luck, or persistence, in finding a Chicago beef buyer named Ramey I could get Amanda Reese off the hook for sure and maybe get Greenough off Howard Blackburn's back too. All Arlo Herring needed was the information. He could do a lot with it.

Four hundred dollars, the man had said. For Greenough it would've been a bargain. Pay a few hundred and get thousands back. A real steal of a price.

Maybe I shouldn't have done it. I'm still not real proud of it. But right then I was not feeling real good toward Mr. Orval Hatcher. I stood and said, "Val, I hope you'll find more mercy from Him than I guess I could give you. Good-bye."

I went back and picked up my rifle and walked down off that hill in the gathering dark.

Behind me Val Hatcher did manage to keep hold of at least some of his pride. I never heard him scream until I was way far away.

CHAPTER 34

Lord, but I'd never felt so tired I don't believe. My feet were dragging as I came around the corner of the house, and I felt three times my age. If it hadn't been for the thought of Manda waiting and worrying inside I think I would have laid down somewhere on that hillside and gone to sleep. If it hadn't been for that, that is, and for the sounds that followed me down from above.

All that tiredness disappeared once I'd rounded the corner. I froze, and a stab of sharp fear jolted through me.

The front door was standing half open.

That door was supposed to be closed and barred until I spoke to her and now it was standing open, and the screen door was unlatched as well.

If I'd gone off and let something happen to her now, when I thought it was all but over, I didn't know what I'd do.

I got over my shock quick enough and stepped fast to the side, pressing tight against the wall while I palmed my revolver and checked to make sure I had reloaded. The long gun I leaned up against the log wall. It would be even more useless here than it had been up on the hill.

I wanted to kick and cuss myself but this wasn't the time. I ducked below the window level and slid forward to the door. Gun ready, I leaned past the doorjamb.

Manda wasn't in the main room.

A smeared trail of blood was. It led from the door back toward the bedroom.

A thousand possibilities went bursting through my mind. All of them were bad.

I wasn't in any humor now for going cautiously slow. As soon as I saw that blood I snatched the door open and rushed inside.

I crossed the big room in a few flying steps and shouldered

straight on into the bedroom with my revolver pushing in ahead of me.

Manda was huddled on the floor at the foot of the bed. She had a chest open on the floor beside her and seemed to be just fine except for looking worried. She looked up at me anxiously.

"Help me, Jude."

I stepped around the bed and saw what she was doing.

Beggar was there on the floor beside her. His hindquarters were matted with old blood and with fresh. It was his blood on the floor, not hers.

"I heard him at the door, Jude. He dragged himself up here somehow. I couldn't leave him out there."

"And you pulled him in here?" I dropped down beside her. The old dog had his head in her lap, but at the sound of my voice he tried to raise it. The end of his chewed-up tail thumped weakly onto the floorboards.

"My medicine chest is in here. Cloth. The things I thought might help. But I don't know what to do, honey. Help me with him."

I touched the big dog's head and then her hand and the great welling of relief and joy I felt was beyond belief, beyond anything I could have imagined. "You're all right?"

"Me? Of course," she said snappishly. "Can you help him?"

"I don't know. Hell, he's lived this long. Now look at me." I took her by the hand, maybe too roughly, and squeezed. "I've got to know you're all right, Manda. Please."

She must have heard the urgency in my voice, though where it came from I wouldn't know. It should have been clear to me that everything was all right now. She turned her hand into mine and covered them both with her right hand. She looked deep into my eyes. "I'm fine, Jude. Really I am." This time she meant what she was saying. It wasn't just some automatic response.

"All right." I smiled at her, and I hoped she could read more there than a few words could say. "Thank you."

I bent over Beggar. He was hurt bad but it had been hours now since he was shot. If he was alive now he might well be by morning too, and if he could make it through the night he might just make it.

"There isn't much we can do but make him comfortable and wait. Try to keep him quiet so the wounds will have a chance to close if they're going to. Do you have any laudanum?"

"Yes. Right here." She reached into the chest and brought out a small brown bottle.

"That should kill the pain and probably make him sleep. Take a little chunk of meat and slice a pocket in it. Pour the stuff in there and we'll give it to him that way."

"How much?"

How much? Good question, that. "About the same as you'd give a kid of the same weight. Eighty, ninety pounds, say."

She nodded as if I'd told her exactly how much to use. Well, that was fine. I wasn't going to confuse her by asking how much I'd just told her to give him. "Take his head while I go get it, Jude."

I slipped close beside her and moved under his head as she pulled away, both of us trying to steady and comfort him. She rose and I said, "One thing you oughta know, Manda. We don't know that he'll live, and if he does he might be ruined."

"I don't care."

"The easy way would be to destroy him now."

"No!" She was firm about it, and no hesitation.

"If he lives and can't walk I've got no way to carry him with me. It'd be a lot harder to put him down then."

"I said no, Jude. I meant it. If we can't find a way to carry him along, why, there's something wrong with us. Now you're *going* to save him, no matter what. We'll worry about the other later."

"'We,' Manda?"

She nodded abruptly, just as firm about that as about trying to save the dog. "Yes, 'we.' I've been thinking while you were gone. When I heard that shooting I thought I was going to die myself, Jude. And then I decided if he killed you, I would find a way to kill him." She looked me in the eyes for a long, quiet time. "Jude, I don't have a thing to offer you except myself. What John and I had, I've lost. You're a damned sheepherder. Sooner or later you'll likely get yourself killed. Until then—if you'll have me—on whatever terms you'd take me—I'm your woman." Her eyes, those deep-green, lovely eyes, fled from mine as if she were afraid of what I would say.

And of course she didn't know yet what had happened up there on that hill or what it would mean to her. To both of us.

I reached up and took her hand and pushed my face against her wrist. The feelings I had then were like an outpouring of condensed warmth. It was a new feeling for me. I liked it.

"Manda . . ." I didn't even know where to start. The grass, the stock cows, a flock of sheep—I knew she wouldn't mind, and I really do like the damn things—they all stretched out before us.

Us. That was the key word there. Us. For the first time it meant more to me than myself and a dog and maybe a horse or two. Us. I liked that. And I didn't even know how to tell her.

She squeezed my hand. "I'll get that laudanum and meat fixed up, honey. We can talk about it then." She smiled. "We'll have lots of time to talk."

Lots of time. I watched her walk away, and I smiled and stroked Beggar's big, scarred head in my lap. Lots of time. Years of it. Lord, but I was blessed, wasn't I?